TRACEY CRINGLE HASN'T GOT A CLUE

A Tracey Cringle
Paranormal Mystery
Book One

A Novel by Sarah Branch

ISBN: 9798612373339

For Lizzie, Katy and Gray.

1

My husband appeared to me for the first time as I was walking to his car. This wouldn't have been so strange ordinarily, but we'd had him cremated three weeks previously. The shock was enough to make me drop the crowbar I had been carrying. It bounced off my big toe and landed on the driveway with a metallic clang. He looked exactly as he had that morning before he left for work; pristine grey suit, crisp white shirt, finished off with a bright cerise tie to show he was confident enough to be in touch with his feminine side. This apparition, however, looked horrified and he held his hands up to stop me walking any further. The last time I had seen him so distressed he'd just opened his credit card bill after one of my more epic shopping trips.

He disappeared as suddenly as he had appeared, leaving me standing by the wheelie bins, slack jawed and big toe throbbing. When I had suitably recovered from the shock, I growled an expletive through clenched teeth whilst gripping my tender toe through my sock. I looked up and down our street; a few cars shot past but there didn't appear to be anyone around who might have witnessed the scene. Did it actually happen?

Grief does strange things to people, particularly when you lose someone as suddenly as I had lost Ben. He just went to work one day and never came home. I guess that's what happens when you attempt to treat a heart attack with ibuprofen and antacids. I did ask the registrar if we could record the cause of death as stupidity. She wasn't amused. Sarcasm is one my preferred coping mechanisms during difficult times, although I haven't yet mastered identifying the most appropriate timing for deployment.

Finding myself left with two teenage daughters to raise, no job of my own and a life insurance pay-out that only just covered our hefty mortgage and a not too shabby funeral, I was facing a financial crisis of the "can't afford to feed my kids" variety. The most sensible option (somehow ahead of getting off my arse and getting a job) was to sell my husband's beloved Audi TT. Unfortunately, I was finding it a struggle to track down the logbook and service history. I had convinced myself that it would be in the glove box, which seemed to be jammed shut, hence the crowbar. Having recovered my composure somewhat, I clicked the key fob and the lights flashed, doors unlocking with a thump. I eased myself onto the passenger seat, leather feeling like ice through my leggings and pulled the door shut against the bitter wind. As I carefully positioned the edge of the crowbar in the slim gap at the top of the glovebox, I felt the temperature drop so fast I was sure I could feel crystals of ice forming on my cheeks. I sat back against the chair, turning my head slowly to my right.

"Hello Tracey." said Ben. He looked startlingly real, except for the unnatural pallor of his skin and blue tinge to his lips. "Please put the crowbar down."

"What the pissing, buggery bollocks..." I whispered irreverently.

"Look, there's just a knack..." the spirit of my dead husband reached over and attempted to grab the handle of the glove box, but it just slipped through his translucent hand and he lurched forward, "Oh crap. Okay well, if you just pull it up as you pull the handle, it will open no problem." Without taking my eyes off him, I reached out a shaking hand groping blindly for the handle. I gave it a little pull upwards and the door sprang open. "Actually, the logbook isn't in there though. It's in the kitchen drawer." He added.

"Are you actually fucking kidding me?" I spoke the words slowly, the shock still snaking through my bloodstream. "All these weeks since you...you...bloody died on me, you complete utter bastard, actually by the way. You could have appeared to me to comfort me and tell me that you loved me. But no, you just pitch up to tell me where the fecking logbook is because you're afraid I'll damage your fecking car!" By the end of the sentence I was actually shouting at him and he had the good grace to look abashed. I was vaguely aware that anyone walking past my driveway right then would just see a mental woman screaming at fresh air as I had almost certainly lost my tiny little mind.

"It's not like that, Trace. You don't just pop up in the afterlife. It takes a while before you can do stuff like this. It's not like I didn't want to come and see you and the kids..." he looked wretched and I felt like an almighty cow. We simmered in our collective misery a moment, but as I turned to talk to him his image started to shimmer and fade away.

"I love you..." he said gently as his ghostly form faded, "...and Trace...don't take a penny under fifteen thousand..." It took me a moment to realise he was talking about the car and I hoped he could see the withering look I gave him before he disappeared completely. I looked at the empty seat beside me, wondering what the hell had just happened. The cool weight of the open glove box resting on my knees reassured me I hadn't imagined everything. I reached out to push it closed.

"Don't forget to mention the heated seats" his voice boomed in my right ear and I jumped.

"Jesus Christ!" I screeched and turned to his faded form which had partially reappeared next to me.

"Or the alloys..." he added as his edges faded out again, "Not a penny under fifteen...." he managed before he disappeared completely again. I sat staring at the empty driver's seat, expecting him to pop back up at any minute, but he didn't.

There was nothing for the shock, but a strong cup of tea with two sugars, half a packet of Hob Nobs and some Seventies disco funk at maximum volume. It seemed to do the trick and I managed to start functioning like a reasonably capable adult within the hour, getting the Audi up for sale on an auction website before getting showered and into clean clothes for the first time since the funeral. The prospect of my late husband observing me from the afterlife was a catalyst to start getting my shit together, although it created a fresh new anxiety on an entirely new level altogether.

I set about making the house the standard of cleanliness and tidiness Ben had insisted upon when he got home and wanted to put his feet up after a long week doing whatever executive things he did for a living. I genuinely had no idea. As long as I knew the bills were paid and there was enough for a decent holiday once a year, I could quite happily keep up my end of the bargain mothering and house-wifing to ensure my family felt looked after and happy. But then Ben had ruined our cosy little existence by going and dying on me. The responsibility of managing the family finances hit me like a blind buzzard, going at full speed. I'd scraped a D in maths at GCSE, so the added joy of dealing with probate was a completely fresh hell, but thankfully a relatively brief one.

So, there I was, four weeks from the horrific day my husband dropped dead at work, with approximately three pounds and twenty-five pence in my bank account, one credit card steaming fast towards it's credit limit and two hungry teenagers to feed. Despite Ben's most recent last wishes I had priced the Audi cheap to get some cash in, out of sheer desperation. Perhaps it would encourage Ben to reappear. I had so many questions I needed to ask him. I really wanted to ask if he was happy with his funeral. Was 'Staying Alive' the right track to use as the coffin was carried to the front of the church? I added a little dance, so that the pallbearers took a few steps backwards at the "ah, ah, ah..." bits based on a very drunken conversation we had had many years ago. I really couldn't tell if Ben had been joking when he'd suggested it, so I'd opted to carry out his wishes to the letter, just in case. My mother in law had been apoplectic with rage at the wake. According to her, the antics had prevented her from mourning the passing of her darling son in a suitably reverent way.

As usual everything simply had to be about her.

She'd made a complete scene at the undertakers when we'd gone to view the body. Wailing like a banshee, she flung herself over Ben's poor corpse. I'd been stood in the corner observing her melodrama and rolling my eyes. In an attempt at humour I had whispered to the attendant "If she carries on like this, she won't be getting an invite to my next wedding...ha ha ha" This had not gone down well. Literally no one in the funeral industry has a sense of humour. Who knew?

What didn't surprise me was that I hadn't heard from any of my in-laws since the funeral. I followed their self-serving cries for attention on social media with great interest, but apparently, I was outside of their sphere of interest. It didn't bother me at all. I was just struggling to find a new level of normality for my familial brood, or rather what was left of it. Teenage girls are very good at putting on a show and between the general teenage angst and hormones it had been impossibly difficult to assess how they were coping with the death of their father.

My eldest, Sophie, seemed to have adopted a mothering role, flapping around me and her younger sister trying in her teenage naivety to somehow make everything okay again. She had always had a bit of a maternal streak and I could easily see her having a horde of her own children eventually. Far too sensible and grown up for her fifteen years, she soldiered on through her own grief preferring to focus on others around her. This was much to the irritation of her sister, Becky, who absolutely did not want to be mothered by anyone.

The rows in the previous two weeks had measured eight point two on the Richter scale and were only mildly less destructive. I had urged Sophie to back off a little and let Becky cope with her grief in her own way, so she had instead busied herself by looking after me. I felt I deserved a little looking after by that stage, so I let her crack on. We could figure things out properly and settle into our new family dynamic when the dust had settled. It did worry me how I would be able to be there for the girls and do all the things I was used to doing, when I had to actually work for a living.

With a dramatically laboured sigh, I cracked open my ancient laptop, manically refreshing my emails to see if there was interest in the Audi. As I was about to search for local part time jobs my phone beeped. I froze for a moment, trying to sense if Ben might be about. How could I know he wasn't watching even when he didn't show himself to me? The hairs on the back of my neck stood up in response, but I couldn't tell if that was in anticipation of an appearance or if it meant he was nearby. I called out his name to the empty kitchen but got nothing in response and felt both relieved and a little bit miffed. I picked up the phone. Just another message from my mum asking if I'd found the sandwich toasting machine that I'd borrowed off her nearly a decade a go yet. I flung my mobile down and rested my head in my hands, trying to make sense of what was going on. My husband was dead, but he was still here, in a manner of speaking. Did that mean he would always be watching over me? Even when I was on the toilet pooping or plucking out my chin hairs? Christ, that was worse than him being gone forever and yet, I wondered when I would get to see him again. Would it be today, or would I have to wait days or weeks or years? Maybe never. He'd just popped back to sort out the car and then that was it. Whilst I wouldn't have blamed him, that would have seriously pissed me off.

When the phone rang ten minutes later, I was reluctant to pick it up. I'd been harangued by "well-wishers" and rubberneckers, in particular those who seem to treat a death as some kind of opportunity for a bit of attention for themselves. They were always easy to spot, sidling up close to me with their false empathy. Vultures. I eventually answered with a grumpy "Hello." The nice man from the supermarket explained that he could not deliver my online shopping as my card had been declined. My stomach hit the floor, but I was too depressed even to cry. My last lifeline, my only remaining credit card (the one with the miniscule limit and monstrous interest rate), was maxed out.

"I don't have any other way to pay" I muttered miserably.

"Oh. Umm...would you like me to cancel the order for you madam?" he asked with a note of panic to his voice. I suspected this didn't happen to him much and I started to sob.

"Yes please." I managed to say before hanging up and resting my head on the kitchen counter to have a good, old-fashioned cry.

Just as I was hoping my tears might flood the surface of the breakfast bar and literally drown me in my own misery, the doorbell rang. Wiping dripping snot along the sleeve of my cardigan, I staggered like a drunk towards the front door, preying it wasn't a well-meaning friend or neighbour come to check in on me. I might be inclined to get sweary-shouty at them. As I neared the door, the pungent smell of cheap aftershave assaulted my streaming nostrils and immediately reassured me that this was no well-wisher. No, this was my brother in law, Trevor. I opened the door to find him leaned against the frame, an unlit cigarette dangling from his bottom lip. His leather jacket gaped open to accommodate a perfectly spherical beer gut which looked like it had been glued on to his otherwise lean, tall frame. He raised an eyebrow at me and snapped up the cigarette placing it behind his ear.

In the time it took for him to complete this attempt at an alluring gesture, I was thinking fast; should I tell him about the food shopping and dismal state of my financial affairs? I could ask him for a loan, but I was certain he was creepy enough to expect something in return for the favour. If I kept quiet, what were my options for getting the kids fed that night? I could have applied for every credit card on the planet, but my credit rating was dreadful and anyway, even if I applied straight away it would take a week for the card to arrive in the post. I could have insisted that we were going to have an "austerity" themed menu for the week and taken the girls out foraging for wild mushrooms and berries. They seriously couldn't whine any more than they normally did at my mealtime offerings. Oh God how can my life have actually come to this, I thought to myself and involuntarily burst out crying. Again.

"There now sweet-cheeks, no need for those tears" he said giving me double guns. Then to my horror, Trevor leaned forward to hug me, encapsulating me in his arms and pressing my face against the ancient smelly leather of his jacket. I'd managed to avoid any form of physical contact with this man for the best part of two decades, so this came as both a shock and a blow. The pungency of his liberally applied aftershave hit the back of my throat and I started to gag, giving my crying a sobbing quality that only made him hug me harder. Soon I couldn't tell if the tears were of sadness or the vanilla scented vapours melting my eyeballs. I managed, with some effort to peel myself away from Trevor, and led him into the house. We turned into the lounge and as I sat back on the couch, he sat so close next to me, he was practically sitting on my lap. He pulled me even closer to him with an arm around my shoulders.

"Come on now..." he muttered. It took several deep shuddering gasps before I could speak properly.

"Supermarket just called." I said eventually after sniffing back a globule of snot, "They're cancelling my shopping..." I was crying again but trying to fight it so I could get the words out, "Card was declined" I finally managed.

"Leave this with Trevor. I will see what I can do." he gave a theatrically condescending wink and whipped out his mobile, a flip-phone affair from the early nineties. Feeling wretched, and slightly manipulative (it truly wasn't my intention to ask for his help) I fetched my own phone to give him the order details so he could phone the call centre back and pay for my food shop. Within minutes, he was waving about his Gold Mastercard and had settled the bill. I sat with my hands pressed between my knees perched on the end of the couch feeling like a naughty schoolgirl being bailed out of trouble and worried about the consequences of relying on Trevor for help. Maybe I had judged him too harshly.

Ben's older brother had always been an underachiever; never in gainful employment but he somehow always seemed to have more money than us. He was a serial bachelor having managed to avoid the trap of matrimony although he still had at least three children (that we knew of anyway) all by different mothers. We'd generally avoided spending time with him at all costs, not out of snobbery, but simply because he would make everyone feel a bit dirty just by being present in the room. A sort of wheeler-dealer, Del-Boy sort, if Only Fools and Horses had been set in a correctional facility for serial sex offenders.

Just as he was finishing the call, having referred to the call handler as "princess" and "Little Lady" several times, I returned to the lounge with a cup of tea for myself and my unlikely saviour. I took the opportunity to sit opposite him on the corner sofa, feeling more comfortable out of touching distance.

"Thank you, Trevor. I really appreciate your help and I promise I will pay you back as soon as the Audi sells." Trevor raised an eyebrow and looked over my shoulder through the lounge window to the gleaming silver convertible on the driveway.

"You know...I know a guy who could help you shift that pretty quick. And for cash too." He leaned forward, his elbows rested on his knees and fixed me with an intense stare. I guessed there was something in it for him and I squirmed trying desperately to think of a way to extricate myself from his offer.

"Thanks, but actually there is someone coming round to take a look at it this afternoon, actually." I hastily sipped my tea and watched to see if he'd bought it.

"Oh...I should stick around and make sure he doesn't rip you off."

"No!" I said too loud and too fast, "It's one of Ben's old workmates." I lied again. I was getting good at fibbing. "Thank you though, for the offer." He nodded slowly. I thought for a moment he might be on to me, but he seemed satisfied with what I had said and sat right back in his seat getting nice and comfortable. Shit.

"How are my cracking little nieces getting on?" he clocked Sophie's school photo resting on the fireplace. "Fuck me!" he spluttered his tea, "Not so little anymore eh?! Turning out to be a little fox." He stroked his trouser legs in a way that made me dangerously nauseous and very angry. Ben chose this moment to materialise in the corner of the room, although I suspected he could have been there for some time listening in to our conversation. "She must be about the same age as Terry by now?"

"She's fifteen, so a year younger I think." I said, trying hard to remain cheerful in spite of the fact his face was starting to piss me off more than normal. It was the kind of face that is neither handsome nor ugly but gives the impression of a person who is overwhelmingly stupid; a dribbles-on-his-chin, vacant, slightly cross-eyed kind of stupid. Occasionally however, he had the focused look of a predator about him. A sexual predator that is.

"Nice" he said and my skin crawled. "Terry is talking about coming to live with his old pa now he's done with school. Cracking lad he is. Like a son to me."

"Trevor. He is your son."

"Yep. Just like a son." He gazed off wistfully. I noticed the room was growing cold and I checked to see if Trevor had noticed, but he was lost in some idiotic reverie. I sneaked a look back at Ben who was pacing angrily in and out of the far wall. I couldn't speak to him or Trevor would have me sectioned, so I just watched as Ben stopped and grasped his hand around a cheap vase his mother had bought me last year for Christmas. His brow furrowed in concentration. I saw the vase shudder gently as his grip gained traction. He glared at Trevor with triumphant rage as the vase launched across the

12

room at Trevor's head.

Trevor yelped and, to my eternal disappointment, dodged it successfully. It smashed on the wall behind his head.

"Did you...did you see that Trace?!" he shouted jumping up from his seat, knocking his mug of tea off the arm of the chair in his haste.

"I know, that's crazy. What just happened? I don't even know...what just happened..." I said but he was already rushing to the front door, "Oh, you're going so soon. What a shame!" I shouted my thanks at him as he hurried up the driveway. By the time I returned to the living room, Ben had disappeared.

2

"Ewww...what is that rank smell?" Becky wrinkled her freckled nose so dramatically I worried her face would invert.

"Your Uncle Trevor popped round today." I said.

"I'm sorry to hear that," said Sophie looping her arm around me in mock sympathy, "are you ok Mum?" I nodded pathetically and tried not to smile.

"What did that creepy old pervert want?" Becky asked, her cynical little face betraying her distrust.

"I think he just wanted to check we were ok." It struck me that I didn't know why he really came round in the first place, but it was unlikely to be anything quite so altruistic.

"Oh God, he wasn't coming on to you was he Mum?" Becky said aghast and Sophie paused rummaging through the snack cupboard to stare at me mouthing a silent 'Oh My God'.

"Oh now, don't be so mean girls. It wouldn't be so bad if your old mum shacked up with Uncle Trevor now would it?" They both squealed in horror and I tried not to laugh, "He's not so bad. Especially if we washed him. He'd come up nice after a hot shower and scrub down with a wire brush and some Dettol."

"Eww!" shouted Becky.

"Oh, he absolutely is that bad Mum. You can do so much better!" added Sophie.

"Aww...fanks you two." I smiled, feeling genuine pride and love for my daughters. I wasn't sure I would have survived the past few weeks without them by my side. Not that I ever expected any different, but they truly were growing up to be incredible young women. There's always a danger when embarking in procreation that you might find yourself raising a complete arsehole for offspring, although I liked to think that outcome was generally reserved for people who were arseholes themselves. Either way, Ben and I had been supremely lucky in that our kids were turning out to be good people.

I felt a sudden pang of guilt; should I tell them that I had seen their father? It might have been a comfort to them to know that their Dad was still about and watching over all of us. But then, I couldn't tell if or when he would be back or how they would react. Also, I had to consider whether they would experience the same clench inducing anxiety whilst on the loo, never knowing when he might just pop up. I decided I would wait and see if he turned up again and try and discuss it with him then. I needed to know if this was some strange transitional haunting or if he would be hanging around for the rest of our lives, and more importantly how I felt about that prospect. He had once joked that when he died, he wanted to be stuffed and positioned on the sofa, so we never forgot about him. Clearly that had been unfeasible, as the undertakers had explained to me, and I hoped that Ben would not be too angry about that.

Becky removed a chocolate digestive from her

mouth to plant a kiss on my cheek and before stuffing it whole into her mouth and skulking off upstairs with the rest of the packet tucked under her arm. Her sister sidled up to me for her kiss, taking the opportunity to remind me that she was approximately one inch taller than me. I was only mildly terrified about how on earth I was going to raise these two all by myself. It occurred to me for the first time since Ben died that I was going to have to potentially finance two university careers in the coming years, which jolted me to continue my job search.

While Sophie crashed about making a start on dinner, I opened up my laptop and started my first job search in over seventeen years. My CV was depressingly brief, and I wondered if I should just focus on the kind of jobs that didn't require a CV at all. Most of the vacancies online appeared to be for seasonal work in the lead up to Christmas and I wasn't sure if that would really solve anything. I found a pretty safe supermarket checkout job and calculated the wages. Even if I got the highest hourly rate on offer and worked a forty-hour week, I would be earning less than half what Ben had brought home each month. Oh wait, I thought, and that doesn't even take into account the tax and all that gubbins they would be taking off. I guessed that I wouldn't have to be earning as much as he had, given the mortgage was now paid off, but I still had bills to pay, children to raise and a lifestyle to uphold. I looked at my chipped nails and briefly mourned what it seemed would be my last ever manicure.

Thoroughly depressed, I slammed the laptop shut. I'd had enough for one day and hoped that a better solution would present itself in the morning. If I could just sell the damn car, that would give me some breathing space.

"You ok Mum?" I looked up to see Sophie watching me, looking concerned, although I conceded it might just be that she had drawn on her eyebrows a little wonky that morning. It happened occasionally.

"Yes love." I said with forced enthusiasm. "Are you ok?" She smiled brightly and I knew she was putting on her own act for my benefit. That's my girl, I thought grimly.

"Yep. I'm fine." She busied herself chopping up an onion, suddenly intensely focused on her task. "I mean…I miss Dad and sometimes I feel sad." I slipped off my seat and stood behind her, wrapping my arms around her shoulders. Soon I felt thick heavy tears drop onto my forearm and I hugged her a little tighter. We were all getting a bit weary of tears and sadness and yet it still kept coming. All we could do was keep on holding one another until our grief faded and hope that day came sooner rather than later.

Later that evening when the girls were in their bedrooms staring into the electronic abyss that was their mobile phones, I lay in bed frantically refreshing the emails on my own mobile, praying for some interest in the car. I could feel the panic rising up through my gullet, my heart rate set to a steady thirty billion beats per second. Stressing about money was a completely new thing for me. Call me a pampered princess but worrying about paying the bills was entirely Ben's domain and I couldn't help feeling a little angry with myself for not taking an interest or doing more to feather our nest sooner. In fairness to me I had attempted to get a job…once, but Ben put his foot down. He had been adamant. He would not risk his own career to be pitching in with childcare during the school holidays. As a result, I had spent the past few years since the girls started secondary school bored out of my tiny little mind, which had prompted me to find new pursuits to fill the time. Now I had neither the time, nor the money, nor the energy to be doing anything other than mothering and fretting about money.

As I refreshed for the hundredth time, I felt the air around me grow colder and although I couldn't confess to enjoying the experience, it was becoming oddly familiar. I looked across the bed, to see Ben fully formed floating a foot above the covers staring at me. I yelped, jumped up lost my balance on the edge of the bed and rolled straight off landing on the floor with a thump. Within seconds the girls had burst into my room, bleary eyed but concerned.

"Mum, are you ok?" Sophie asked peering over the side of the bed to where I lay tangled in the covers which I had dragged with me.

"Yep." I gave them a thumbs up and then clambered to my feet. "Absolutely fine. Just fell out of bed." I looked to Ben and he was still there, head turned towards the girls. Their faces were sleep crumpled and frowning at me, but there was no sign that they had picked up on their father's presence. I felt a sudden, desperate urge to tell them that their father was there in the room and if they just looked a little closer, they might be able to see him, but the words refused to form in my mouth. They silently accepted my explanation and shuffled back off to their rooms. I straightened the covers and climbed back onto the bed next to the ghost of my late husband.

"Don't get me wrong, I love having you back, but could you not fecking scare the shit out of me like that?" I felt bad saying it as he stared after our girls and the empty doorway where they had been stood.

"Oh, yeah. Sorry." He said pulling his gaze from the empty doorway to look at me with big, sad eyes. I wanted nothing more in that moment to comfort him, but what good was there in hugging a ghost? And besides, there were things I needed to know.

"Are you always here, watching over us?" I asked as he settled his ghostly countenance on the pillow beside me. I lay down on my own pillow, so we were face to face.

"No. I wish I could." The air surrounding him felt like an arctic breeze on my bare skin and I hunkered down into the covers to stop myself shivering. "When I come down, it's like I'm holding my breath and diving down under water. I can't stay too long, but it gets easier each time and I'll be able to stay longer. At least, that's what they're telling me." I tried to reach out to touch his face, but my hand passed through his cheek like a chill mist.

."I miss you." I said and a tear streaked down my cheek. "I didn't think I would, but I do." We both chuckled quietly.

"I miss you too." His edges were starting to blur.

"Are you alone? On the other side or whatever you call it?" I had to ask him because it had been bothering me.

"No. There are others here."

"Is my granny Ivy there?" I asked, welling up again. He grimaced.

"Err...I haven't checked actually." He looked sheepish. Never one for voluntary familial interactions beyond our little foursome, I suspected he might spend an eternity in the afterlife stealthily avoiding the extended family. "I'll have a look when I get back" he said, and I knew he wouldn't.

"Are there times you are here and watching over us when we can't see you?" At last the question I really wanted to ask. He was starting to fade again, and I could see the mirrored wardrobe door through his face, which gave the curious effect of the reflection of my face being superimposed onto his.

"No, you'll know when I'm about." He said and looked at once implausibly sad.

"Don't go."

"I have to, I'm sorry Trace. I'll be back soon. I promise." He said and then he disappeared completely. I laid onto my back and stared up at the artexed ceiling until my eyes grew weary and the icy edge to the air had left completely. Feeling suddenly very alone, I reached out for my mobile and shot off a text message. Not waiting for a response, I pulled the covers tight around me and drifted off to sleep.

When I woke again, my alarm clock told me it was past three and the room was dark and cold. Colder even than usual and I could see my breath billowing out in thick white clouds. I sat up in bed, instantly wide awake.

"Ben?" I whispered into the empty room. My sleep weary eyes struggled to scan the darkness around me and at first, I couldn't see anything. A gentle creak in the corner of the room barely registered over the sound of my heart thudding in my ears. This felt different to the times that Ben had appeared before and I felt an unwelcome dread rising up from my stomach, constricting my throat. My eyes scanned the dark corner that the noise had come from and struggled to pick out the details of the furniture in that corner of the room; a tall chest of drawers with a vanity mirror on top, a chair to its left piled high with dirty clothes and a tall lamp beside it. No wait, I thought, the chair was in the other corner of the room.

The thin, dark shadow shifted a little and I tensed. A cold drip of sweat slithered down the centre of my spine. The shadow lumbered forward, one step, then two until it levelled with the end of the bed. Closer now I could see it was not so tall, maybe the size of a child and my logical brain worked hard to convince me that this was my own child woken in the night and snuck into my room for cuddles, but I knew that neither of my girls was so small anymore. As the shadow stood by the side of my bed, swaying slightly from side to side, I could feel it watching me its head cocked slightly to one side, staring at me through the darkness before I couldn't take it any longer. Without tearing my gaze away, I reached out to the bedside table and fumbled for the lamp switch, pausing when I found it to consider if I really wanted to see what had come to visit me. I drew a shaky breath and clicked the switch.

Stood by my bed was a young girl, aged about eight or nine. Her long brown hair hung in tangles about her shoulders. Her eyes were shut. As I watched her, she shuffled forward, dragging her feet on the carpet beneath her and my heart lurched. I silently begged her not to come any closer, but she didn't listen. As she approached, I felt the coldness around me thicken and hang off my bare skin like a dead weight. She reached up and pulled her long hair back from her face. Her lips moved but her words barely registered in the shock.

"He took my eyes." She cried as her eyelids snapped open and I saw the red, empty sockets staring back at me.

3

I spent the rest of the night, sleeping in short, snatched stretches. It was the fitful, anxious sleep of someone who has an early morning flight to catch and is terrified of sleeping through the alarm. Around the time the sun started to rise, I managed a deeper more settled slumber, perhaps because I knew there were no shadows left to be hidden in. I woke for the final time that morning, considerably later than I had intended, clambering out of bed long after the girls had both taken themselves off to school, to my shame. I hoped Ben wouldn't pop up before I'd had the chance to get myself showered and respectable, ready to start my job search in earnest by hitting the streets of Alton with my anorexic CV. I'd figured that it might be a better way to scout out the opportunities and communicate my complex needs from future employment to prospective bosses. And by that I meant the need to work only three short (school hour) days a week during term time only, with the flexibility to change days around at short notice, with a decent salary; none of this minimum wage nonsense. I was certain that once they had met me and had a chance to appreciate my charisma and charm, they would be biting my hand off to offer me a job on these terms.

In the shower I daydreamed about heading up my own departmental meeting with colourful Powerpoint presentations and me stood confident and neatly turned out at the front of a board room, my team smiling warmly and cheering as I reached the meeting's climax to a dignified applause. As I dried my hair, I was imagining accepting a big promotion from the company CEO before jumping in my brand-new Range Rover to head home and celebrate with the girls. As I strode into town, head held high and suede boots kicking up dead leaves with every step, I was thinking about retiring at the age of fifty and spending weeks at a time in my holiday home in the West Country drinking prosecco and watching the waves lap up onto a deserted beach. Adamantly ignoring my utter exhaustion, I chose to be inexplicably on top of the world and convinced that this was my turn to shine. Denial is a marvellous thing!

The high street was curiously deserted for a Tuesday morning. The ancient market town of Alton could never be considered a sprawling metropolis, but the eclectic mix of independent boutique shops and high street names was enough to attract a reasonable patronage. To a lazy observer, the high street itself was just a smattering of ugly concrete built according to the seventies code of blocky architecture, that had earned Alton it's place in the British league table of crap towns. If you took the time however, and looked a little closer, you would see hidden amongst the concrete and generic shop fronts, a wealth of crooked timber framed buildings and their taller, grander Georgian neighbours.

I started at the top of the High street, which sat on a steep hill and tried my luck at the artisan coffee place that had just opened up, selling my extensive (if fictitious) business acumen as a star quality for a managerial position that to the best of my knowledge didn't actually exist. The bemused, bespectacled hipster at the counter took my CV, I suspect out of politeness and apologetically informed me that there were no vacancies at present but assured me he would keep my CV "on file". This apparently meant flung under the counter. He did glance at it first though, his brow furrowed and flipped it quickly over to check the back of the paper, which was blank. I decided that he must be some kind of snob and hastily retreated back to the fresh, cool air outside.

There were a few, similar encounters in the smaller, independent shops that scattered the town centre and I decided that I was obviously pitching myself too low. I headed to some of the bigger players, although in this relatively modest town, the pickings were slim. Nevertheless, I persevered handing out several more CVs to similarly perplexed counter staff at Boots, Clarkes and Co-op effectively pitching for the role of store manager, all the while reflecting on the fine line between optimism and delusion. By the time I left the last shop, I was not feeling confident of a call back. I decided to head into one of the chain coffee shops, which was mercifully mostly empty, besides a few flustered middle-class mums with rampant toddlers. At the counter, a spotty youth studiously ignored me for several minutes while she jabbed at the till's computer screen. When she finally looked up at me, her face a picture of blank wonder. I offered a warm smile.

"I was just wondering if you have any job vacancies?" I handed over the second to last tatty piece of paper containing my shameful account of the last two decades of my life. Spotty youth regarded it briefly.

"Have you got any experience as a barista?" she asked in an unexpectedly deep and authoritative voice.

"Sorry...?" I asked and she pointed to her own name badge telling me she was Lottie and she was a Master Barista. I wondered briefly why experience in the field of law might be a requirement to work in a grubby coffee shop.

"A ba-ris-ta" she said loud and slow, as if talking to an extremely deaf, slightly confused elderly lady lacking in mental faculties. "A barista is someone who prepares coffee and coffee-related beverages in a high-quality hot beverage establishment...such as this." She swept her arms about her and I looked about me, not quite sure if she was being a bit sarcastic.

"Oh! Of course. Yes, I have." I've boiled the kettle for a cup of Kenco on many occasion, which is almost certainly not what she meant, but I was not going to mention that to the patronising little madam. "Would it be possible to speak to the manager please?" I said straightening a little to assert myself more effectively. I was suddenly certain I would be this youngster's line manager in no time at all.

"I am the store manager." She said levelling with me. Bollocks I thought. "We don't actually have any vacancies at the moment, but I will keep your CV on file." She added with a snide tone, pushing my CV to one side and pinning it to the counter with a glass jar full of marshmallows.

"Thank you." I said through lightly gritted teeth with a tight smile and then looked at the board over her shoulder. "Anyway, while I'm here, I would like a Black Forest Hot Chocolate, with extra cream and extra chocolate sprinkles. Thank you." My dignity had been restored by the server-customer relationship and I managed to stand a little taller.

"We have to charge extra for double sprinkles." She said deadpan and I slumped back down.

"That's fine." I said before I realised, breaking into a cold sweat, I only had three pounds twenty-five pence in my bank account. At least I had the day before when I'd last checked. The grim spectre of unexpected direct debits had become my arch nemesis. As she hollered my order over her shoulder at another gangly, bored looking youth and jabbed it into the till, I fumbled my wallet out of my handbag with a growing sense of dread and trembling fingers. Flipping open the card section, I surveyed with some sadness the collection of Ben's credit cards that had all been cut off. Just my battered old debit card with its meagre offerings remained able to help me. Unless...feeling a sudden rush of helpless optimism I checked in the pocket where I would normally stuff notes, receipts and lesser used reward cards. There shining back at me as if haloed by manna from heaven was one solitary, green five-pound note. I could have cried with relief, but instead I steadied myself, plucked my tiny saviour out and handed it triumphantly to Lottie the Stroppy barista.

"That's four pounds, twenty-five." She said snatching up the note without making eye contact. I let out an involuntary whimper, feeling my bum cheeks clench. I tried to cover it with a little fake cough and moved swiftly away from the counter to wait for my drink, Lottie's eyes following me all the while, with one eyebrow raised. I couldn't help but pout as she dropped my change into her tip jar. Cow.

By the time I had scurried across to a quiet table with my drink, my blood pressure had just about returned to normal. I decided that this worrying about money business did not suit me at all. In fact, I absolutely loathed it. Silently, I cursed Ben for not increasing his life cover when we moved to Bennett Close and took on a ridiculous mortgage. I should have been grateful that the life insurance had covered the mortgage to be fair, but I wasn't in the mood for gratitude. I buried my face in the cream on top of my drink, hoping it would take the edge off my dismay.

It was two in the afternoon by then and there had been no sign of Ben as yet. I was desperate to ask him about what I saw last night. I looked out onto the street as if I might see him walking past the window or standing on the opposite the side of the street, which I might have done only a few weeks ago. The pavements were filling up with scruffy people in tracksuits, the elderly pulling their wheeled shoppers behind them and the occasional exhausted mum pushing a pram. No sign of my recently deceased husband nor anyone else I might have deemed to be an ally. A white notice in the window of the pub on the opposite side of the road caught my eye.

Downing the dredges of my drink and feeling buoyed by the sugar rush I headed out and crossed the road. It was definitely a job advert for bar staff. My expectations had plummeted to the gutter, so I found the prospect of being a bar wench actually quite appealing. I looked up at the squat facade of The Kings Arms and wondered why, in all the years I had lived in Alton, I had never been into this particular drinking establishment. As I pushed through the front door and my feet stuck fast to the carpet, I started to realise precisely why. By then the barman had already spotted me and looked up from his paper. Turning around and leaving would have been exceptionally rude and so I walked to the bar, feeling the gentle tug of moist carpet against the bottom of my shoes with every step. He was eyeing the slightly crumpled CV in my hand and he stood up, crossing his heavily tattooed arms across his chest.

"Hi, umm hello." I said as brightly as I could muster. "I was just wondering about the job?" I pointed back to the window and he silently followed the trajectory of my finger and then looked back at me.

"You need Pat." he turned to shout over his shoulder. "Pat!" He nodded his head in the direction of a door leading out into the alleyway that ran alongside the pub. Not waiting for a response, he mumbled "He's out back" and returned to his newspaper. I retracted my proffered CV and cagily made my way out into the alleyway, trying not to let my nostrils twitch at the unmistakably pubby aroma of the place.

Pat was considerably younger and thinner than I had anticipated of the landlord of the grubbiest pub in all of Alton (perhaps all of Hampshire). The lick of silver at his temples would have given him a distinguished look in any other setting, but the large brown stain down the front of his yellow polo shirt dispelled any such notions. He extinguished his cigarette and coughed heartily into his hand before reaching out for my CV.

"Hi, I'm Tracey." I said, handing it over reluctantly.

"Good name for a barmaid that." He said with a healthy Hampshire burr, before staring down at my CV and turning it over with a frown. "You worked in a bar before love?" He clumsily folded my CV and jammed it into his back pocket.

"No." I said, having given up trying to sell myself. I wasn't convinced I wanted to work here

28

anyway.

"Right..." he looked me up and down, like a butcher sizing up his prize pig, only to find said pig was suffering from a wasting disease with little to commend itself to the butcher shop window. He seemed to have confused himself by his own appraisal of me, which in turn confused me. "Well thanks for stopping by. I'll be in touch." He added before stepping back into the pub.

On the long walk home, I tried to distract myself by looking longingly at the charming hunched up cottages that lined my route watching the twinkle of Christmas lights within. I'd always been a sucker for those dinky cottages with their little quaint rooms, snug fireplaces and Dickensian-style slum living conditions, because I'm nostalgic like that. Always the voice of reason, Ben had always been quick to scupper my fantasies by pointing out they were cramped, cold and damp, not to mention the horrific cost to maintain a period property. He had always been the ultimate killjoy, but I was surprised I hadn't felt a sense of freedom to do all of the things that I always wanted to do, since he had been gone. It was more like a security blanket had been ripped away and I was completely overwhelmed by the knowledge that I would have to be entirely responsible for my own dreadful decision making from now on.

At the end of Tanhouse Lane the path opened out into the Flood Meadows. Comprising a series of interlinked fields with the River Wey running along its southern edge, it was hemmed in on all sides by housing estates creating a small suburban idyll in the heart of the town. Skeletal trees lined the path that led me home, forming an archway over my head. My mind was still chewing over the prospect of working in the sticky carpeted pub pulling pints. As I hauled my arse up the steep hill leading into our road, I imagined myself in the job centre, greasy haired and despondent begging for my benefit cheques. As I arrived at my house, I was imagining empty cupboards and my children in rags. This day had not ended up the way I had anticipated it would. I let myself into the house and hurled myself onto the couch, pulling a blanket over me.

4

I was woken several hours later by the feeling of someone sitting down on the edge of the couch beside me. I opened my eyes to find that my sister, Immy, had used her spare key to let herself in and make us both a cup of tea. She placed mine on the floor by her feet and took a tentative sip of her own, pushing a wisp of her honey blonde hair that had fallen out of the clip, away from her face.

"Still wallowing are we?" she said, without a hint of sympathy or warmth.

"Wallowing?" I said as I shuffled myself into a sitting position and reached down for my cup. My mouth felt like a rodent had taken up residence. "What would you have me do? Should I be out searching for a new husband already?" She shook her head and gave me a stern look.

"It's far too soon for that. You should probably give it another week or two at least." A sly smile snuck across her face. "But if you are after a consolatory bonk, I can get you set up with a profile on Tinder?" My sister was a committed serial spinster, but that didn't ever mean she was ever on her own. She normally had a string of casual lovers on the go, trading them in

31

whenever she happened to get bored, but staunchly refusing to commit to more than a weekly leg up or two at any one time. Immy would say it was to enable to her to focus on her business; she was a mortgage adviser with a smart office in the centre of town and worked every unsociable hour she could. I had long suspected, to the contrary, that she was simply afraid to settle down.

Immy had been diagnosed with Neurofibromatosis at the age of three, just after I was born. The tell-tale cafe-au-lait spots that littered her back and tummy and arms had seemed innocuous enough, but our local GP had been concerned enough to refer her for tests at the hospital. The diagnosis itself had been a complete non-event. The condition might show no symptoms at all for years, or ever, but the threat of what could develop hung heavy over my family for the rest of our childhood. Immy was eleven when they found a tumour on her brain and the treatment had been aggressive. My brave big sister took a battering but her spirit and strength, it seemed, never wavered. At the age of fifteen when her periods still hadn't started, but the cancer had been defeated, Mum took her back to the doctors. It took a lot of poking and prodding to conclude that Immy had been left infertile by her cancer treatment. She would never admit to it, but I always knew that this was the real reason Immy would never settle down. She was tough as nails my big sister and she wouldn't take any flakiness from me either.

"I'm good thanks." I said, resolutely declining her matchmaking offer, "I doubt there are any eligible gents out there that would be interested in a ropey old bird like me...and if they were, they would probably be ancient old perverts, in which case I would certainly not be interested in them. But more importantly, it is far too soon to even think about things like that! But more important even than that, I just can't be arsed to shave my legs."

"Fair point well made." She said, "Seriously though Trace, you need to get up and get busy. No point moping."

"I have though!" I protested miserably, "I've been out job hunting all day today."

"And?"

"There's nothing. My CV is dreadful and even the bars and shops don't want me serving on the tills. I'm utterly unemployable." It occurred to me then that I could just ask Immy for a job at her place, and judging by the slightly awkward strained look on her face the same had occurred to her, "Don't suppose you..."

"No," she cut me off, "I'm fully staffed Trace, I'm sorry. You know I would in a heartbeat if I could. Surely there must be something that you can do. Maybe you could start your own business, cleaning or ironing or something?" She had a point. Working for myself would give me the flexibility I needed to be around for the girls and would give me enough spare time to have a bit of a life for myself. The idea stuck and grew on me fast.

"That's not a bad idea." I said as my sluggish brain chewed on it a little. Immy looked massively relieved and chugged down some more tea. Her phone beeped and she dug it out of her purse, looked at the message and grinning, typing out a hasty message.

"What's this poor sap's name then?" I asked. She was still smiling and looking at her phone, tapping out a reply with both thumbs so I wondered if she'd heard me.

"Alex" she said eventually in a slightly dreamy tone, not noticing my face had drained of all colour as my stomach sunk to my knees.

"How did you meet him?" I tried to come across laid back. It can't be the same Alex I thought desperately as I waited for her to tear herself away from the text volley they seemed to have going. He wouldn't do that to me.

"He did some plastering in our office. He's delightfully...practical. He's coming round to tile my downstairs loo next week."

"Sounds like a euphemism. He's a builder then?" I had to check.

"Yep." She finally looked up from her phone, "Oh relax it's not your Alex. Paranoid much? My Alex is a lot more practical. He has the hands of a man who's done real work all his life, all rough and big and strong, if you know what I mean?"

"Okay, too much information, thank you." I interjected quickly before she could incriminate me further, my face turning deep red. She chuckled to herself and turned back to her phone. I sighed deeply into my mug but then tensed as I spotted Ben across the room. How long had he been there, I wondered? His face was serious, and his gaze fixed on the carpet in front of him. I couldn't tell from his expression if he'd spotted a nasty stain or if he was thinking about the conversation Immy and I had just had. He was just as infuriatingly hard to read when he was alive. I looked to Immy to see if she had noticed the change in atmosphere. She shivered slightly but was otherwise engrossed in her phone. "So, could this be the one...this Alex?" I asked.

"Oh God no." She wrinkled her nose and laughed. "No, I'm far too young to be settling down." Her comment was tongue in cheek, but it was a running joke, so I didn't pass comment, "He's pretty handy for the time being and really rather handsome. He's got one of those hipster beards and dark blue eyes, oh and the muscles. Not the steroid-pumped, rippling hunk type of muscles. The lean strength of a man accustomed to manual labour, you know?" I shook my head.

"Nope." Ben was an entirely sedentary creature, collapsing on the sofa after a long day staring at the computer, with the soft doughy tummy of a man that consumed far too many service station sandwiches. I had loved it and wouldn't have changed him for the world. If only we'd known the impact all that saturated fat and salt was having on his body. He was still pretty slim, apart from his beer belly, but you would never have thought to look at him that he was about to drop dead of a heart attack at the age of forty-three. The doctors had said he had an alarming amount of internal fat. It seemed unfair we hadn't had any warning or opportunity to frog march him down to the gym to get in shape. The whole situation was beyond cruel.

Ben's ghost looked up and met my eye. I could see Immy turn and follow my gaze in the corner of my eye.

"Everything ok?" she asked.

"Yep, sorry was just thinking about Ben." We both sighed in unison. My sister wrapped her arms around my waist and lay down on top of me. Everyone close to me had struggled, not quite knowing how to cope with my grief, without exception. My mother for example, had taken to coming around the house and cleaning manically. Anything to avoid sitting down and talking to me or any form of physical contact, like a reassuring hug. It wasn't her fault though, she just struggled to deal with her own grief, on top of knowing how to comfort me in mine. Mum and Ben had been pretty close, although she would never have admitted to it, Mum had always yearned to have a son of her own. I knew this because when I had had two girls of my own, she had urged me for years to have another, trying to convince me that I would regret it if I didn't at least try for a boy. I didn't try for a boy and I didn't regret it in the least, but it didn't stop her being disappointed in me, although in fairness to her, she had been severely disappointed in me long before that.

The sound of the front door opening prompted Immy to sit up and I noticed Ben had started to slip away. Sophie and Becky bustled into the room, dumping schoolbags at the door and kicking shoes off.

"Aunty Immy!" Sophie squealed and Immy stood, sweeping her up in an embrace, kissing the top of her head as she did so. Having waited patiently for her turn, Becky slipped into the space Sophie had left. As she disengaged from her aunty, Sophie flumped down on the edge of the sofa by my legs and lay her head on my chest.

"How'd the job hunting go, Mum?" she muffled into the blanket.

"Not great. But I have a few ideas, so don't fear. I will get something sorted." I said trying to sound mildly less clinically depressed than I felt.

"How about the car?" Becky asked, from deep within Immy's embrace.

"Oh, good point." I said and reached out to check my phone, carefully angling the screen away from Sophie's field of vision. I refreshed my emails. "Nope, nothing. I think I'm just going to have to reduce the price a bit." I said loudly, hoping that Ben would hear and think that I had tried to get the price he wanted for the damn car. He had by then completely dissipated into the air. I guessed that he found it harder to be around the girls as he rarely hung around for long when they were home. It must have still hurt too much for him. It certainly hurt me to see him watching them, the mournful look on his face was too much to bear. With a few clicks I had reduced the listed price of the car by a couple of grand. Hopefully that would nudge things along a bit and save us from having to be bailed out by dribbling Trev again.

"Right, who fancies pizza for tea" shouted Immy and the girls cheered. Before I could object, she'd whipped out her mobile and her credit card and the girls were salivating over hot dog stuffed crust and cheesy nachos. I sat back and smiled, loving the feeling of being just ever so slightly taken care of. I knew deep down, however, it was a sticky plaster over a gaping wound and my mind wouldn't rest until I had the solution to our money woes sorted.

It was not until several hours later, with a belly full of starch and carbohydrates, the idea struck me and all at once I knew it was the only and best way I could get out of this mess. All I had to do was figure out how to summon the spirit of my dead husband.

5

I was about to drift off to sleep when Ben finally showed up. It was the fifth time he had appeared to me in two days, but only the third opportunity I had had to speak to him properly.

"Ah! Just the person." I said springing up in bed, suddenly wide awake again, and taking him by surprise for once. "I need to run something by you."

"Oh, hello dear and how are you?" he said sarcastically as his shimmering form settled itself onto the end of the bed.

"Yes, yes, I'm fine. I've got an idea. Just bear with me before you decide on anything though." He looked at me, utterly perplexed and silently nodded.

"Is this about my car?" he asked suddenly, and I shot him a venomous look.

"Give over about the fecking car already."

"Yep, fine, sorry. Go for it."

"Right, ok. So, I'm having a bit of difficulty finding a job, on account of my having no skills or qualifications or any real talent for anything actually." He nodded in agreement (git) and shimmied closer to me on the bed.

"It's just your first day job-hunting. Don't get

down about it. It'll just take a little time. You'll find something better than what was on offer at those dives you went to today."

"Oh. You know about that then." I was taken aback. Just how often was he hanging about watching me. "So how does that work anyway, are you watching me all of the time...or what? How's that work?" I hoped he couldn't see my cheeks colouring.

"Like I said, I dive back down when I can, see what's going on. Check in on the people I love." He shrugged, like it was the most normal thing in the world. "Why do you ask?"

"So, can you see into the future?" he shook his head. "Nope, don't think so anyway."

"How about the past?" I ventured.

"Nope, not that either." I let out a quiet sigh of relief and hoped that he didn't hear it. "But I can speak to other spirits and if they've been paying attention, they will know about stuff that has happened in the past. Like my Great Aunt Milly, she had loads to say when I crossed over. Did you know that your mum was pregnant between you and your sister? She lost the baby quite late in the pregnancy. Shame really. Apparently, it was a boy too." Poor mum, I thought but I couldn't suppress the anxiety bubbling up in my chest. "Why do you ask anyway?" He fixed me with an intense stare and for a moment I was convinced he knew.

"I'm just curious, you know, I wondered how those psychic mediums work. The ones that tell fortunes and all that stuff." I needed to get back on topic.

"I'm not sure" he said thoughtfully, "I should imagine that most of them are fakes, but I guess some of them could be making contact with someone on the other side."

"Like I am with you, you mean?"

"Yeah, I guess so," he frowned suspiciously at me then, "Why? Where are you going with this?"

"Well, I was talking to Immy this afternoon and she made an interesting suggestion...that I should consider working for myself. She actually suggested doing cleaning or ironing, but I already checked online and there tonnes of mums already doing that in Alton and the money is dreadful. I'm not working my manicure off for a pittance."

"You can't afford to have a manicure anymore, but yeah, okay. What else could you do though?" he asked the question in earnest and he looked genuinely stumped, leaving me more than a little wounded. Did he consider me so completely useless? I needed to keep him on side however, so I held back my raging indignity.

"I could...become a psychic medium..." I said the words gingerly and registered his shock with a wince.

"That's nuts!" he shouted, and I wanted to tell him to hush until I remembered the girls probably couldn't even hear him. "How would that even work? I don't even know where to start."

"We can figure all of that out. But you know that some mediums charge up to sixty pound for a half hour session. All we have to do is track down some ancient busybody of a dead relative, get them to tell us some obscure family secrets and then tell them they are going to meet a tall dark stranger or something like that. Bosh! Sixty quid. Easy as."

"Trace, it sounds anything but easy. Like, how would I find these relatives? What would you even tell them about their future? Where are you going to find these gullible idiots?"

"Clients!", I tutted at him "I'll find a way. Please promise me that you will at least consider it, Ben. I don't want to spend my life working for Pat in the stickiest carpeted pub in town."

"I don't think you need to worry about that." Ben said quietly.

"Oh, did I not get that job either?" I was incredulous. I would have been great for that place. "Thanks for breaking it to me gently!" I was in a full-blown strop. Not only had he pooh-poohed my plans for getting solvent again, but he had taken away my last hope of gainful employment. I half wished that he would bugger off and immediately felt dreadful. I looked up at him perched on the bed with a look of penetrating sadness on his opaque face. I could see that his edges were starting to fade again, and I started to doubt the feasibility of my own plan. If he could only manage ten minutes with me, I wasn't sure that this plan could even work. It was straight back to square one.

"I'm going to have to go soon." He said quietly and I nodded. I didn't want him to go, but the fact I couldn't grab him and hug him hard was slowly killing me. Then I suddenly remembered.

"Ben, before you go," I asked urgently, "do you know anything about the little girl?" He furrowed his brow.

"No. What little girl?" He looked a little concerned.

"I woke up and saw a little girl by the side of the bed." He shook his head. His form was fading fast, "She had no eyes." He looked stunned, eyes wide looking urgently around him at the room, as he faded

41

completely into the thin air, leaving me alone in the bedroom shuddering against the cold.

6

The temptation to fester in bed the next day was overwhelming. After all, what was there to get up for? The girls were pretty much looking after themselves, getting themselves off to school without any input from me, and making a conscientious effort not to wake me. I had no job and therefore by association no cash with which to take myself off out shopping to distract myself. I didn't even have any chocolate hobnobs to inhale as I watched daytime tv on the couch, so I lingered on in bed until my back hurt and my brain ached from entertaining myself with my own sallow thoughts.

There was a potential buyer coming to look at the car at eleven, but that did little to enthuse me and it was only the thought of another begging session with Trevor that managed to coax me out of the bed at ten forty-five. I jumped in and out of the shower in record time, twisted my hair up into an extremely messy bun and pulled on the stained jeans, tee-shirt and one of Ben's old holey jumpers; an ensemble that had been trotted out for four days in a row, but I wasn't ashamed and I was reasonably sure it didn't smell. Well not too bad anyway. The doorbell went just as I was slumping down the last two steps, scuppering my intentions of a hasty breakfast.

The potential buyers name was Hugo, but the man at the door dispelled all preconceptions that I had had of him on first sight, which would teach me to be so judgmental. I had expected a cashmere and corduroy clad chinless wonder. Tall and gormless with a vacant, skinny blond wife hanging off his arm. Instead, a short rotund man spun around, guiltily hiding his cigarette behind his back as I answered the door. His friendly smile exposed a small but noticeable gap between his two front teeth. I wasn't sure how this changed things, but I instantly relaxed in his company.

"Hullo!" he said, his Hampshire accent thick like he'd spent his whole life on a farm. A posh farm at that, "I've come about the car."

"Hi, you must be Hugo." I said as enthusiastically as I could muster, reaching out to shake his proffered chubby hand. It was horribly damp, and I immediately wished he had at least had the good grace to wipe it off on his trousers first. "I'll just grab the keys." I said as I headed back into the house, re-emerging to find him admiring Ben's pride and joy with almost erotic pleasure. I watched with dismay as he gently ran his hand across the front of the bonnet and sighed.

"She's a beut." He muttered as I stood beside him. I've never entirely understood the excitement people feel about cars. They are just simple hunks of metal that get you about, mostly when they are not being dickheads and breaking down. My own rusting Corsa had sat neglected on the driveway, largely ignored since Ben died, although it had rarely been used before that, bar the weekly run to the supermarket or the odd trip to visit my parents. I hadn't visited them since the funeral. They had, presumably been too busy working to come to me and I hadn't wanted to bother them either. Dad was a magician, a small-town celebrity in his own right and invited to perform at any self-respecting high-brow event within ten miles. My mother was his beautiful assistant although we had managed to convince her to retire her magenta leotard just ahead of her sixty-fifth birthday on the grounds her camel toe was becoming more prominent that was considered decent in polite society. It had been a battle though, not unlike when the police confiscated her fantail feather train when it put a small child in a neck-brace at a ninetieth birthday party a few years previous. She was a formidable and tenacious woman, my mother and she most certainly did not like being told what to do. I would have to go and check on them soon, but first I needed to sell this bloody car so I could afford petrol to put into my own bloody car.

I winced as Hugo took a kick at one the tyres. I thought that was some kind of urban legend about tyre kickers, I mean what did it actually tell you about a car besides confirming that the tyres were definitely not about to fall off. I looked around to check if Ben had materialised; he hadn't and I didn't expect him too. It seemed he couldn't bear to see the car go. I on the other hand was just visualising the big pile of cash that would be all mine, once I'd offloaded it onto this guy. I could tell from Hugo's body language that he had a serious boner for Ben's car, he was just furiously trying to think of reasons to knock me down on price.

"How about we take her out for a drive?" I said with a smile, handing out the car key. Hugo was momentarily rendered speechless with excitement. Within seconds we were buckled up and ready to go, although he delayed starting the car so that he could stroke the dashboard affectionately. To be fair I vaguely recalled Ben doing something similar when the car had first been dropped off, but I still rolled my eyes so hard I think I caught a glimpse of my own brain.

As he reached for the keys, I had a pang of anxiety realising that I hadn't even tried to start it since Ben had died, but the engine sprang to life eliciting a nauseating grin from Hugo. He wiped his sweaty hands on his jeans before reverently gripping the steering wheel. A strangled squeak from the back seat made me cast a look over my shoulder. Ben was sat, hunched up on the back seat looking implausibly sad.

"He's not good enough for my baby. Can't you hold out and sell her to someone who's not on a register?" he said miserably. I smiled and turned back to Hugo. Despite all of his gentleness with the car so far, he jammed his foot hard onto the clutch and scraped it into gear with so much force I thought the gearstick was going to snap off in his hand. I couldn't bear to look back at Ben who was no doubt crying tears of deep emotional pain. The strangled, guttural noises coming from the back of the car were enough to confirm he was a tortured soul. It wasn't long into the journey before I started to wish I'd just let him drive the car off by himself. His driving etiquette was beyond aggressive; effectively everyone was a useless twat, most pedestrians elicited a two fingered salute and he even stopped the car and reversed back a good 10 metres to wind down my window and hurl a tirade of abuse at one poor cyclist who had had the misfortune to be alive (his only crime that I could divine). Despite this and the fact I had spent most of the drive gripping onto the door handle and edge of my seat fearing for my life, he presented me with the most charming and delightful of smiles as we screeched to a halt outside of my house.

"I've got to have her. She's perfect." He said breathlessly.

"Nooooooooo." Wailed Ben.

"Fantastic," I said," will you be paying cash or bank transfer?"

"Nooooooooo." Wailed Ben, "There has to be someone else! Please!"

"I will organise a transfer," he said adding with a flourish, "for the full asking price!" There was no disguising the child-like delight on his face and I felt a slightly warm feeling at having brought a bit of happiness to another human being, even if he was undoubtedly a bit of a sex pest.

"Nooooooooo." Wailed Ben, sobbing into the leather upholstery on the back seat. We sat a moment with our phones out as the funds were transferred into my bank account, and I had to admit that the sight of such a handsome sum in my account made me (and I've no doubt my bank manager) sigh with relief. It felt like four weeks of almost constant pressure and stress and had been lifted from my shoulders. I could finally try and reassemble some form of life for myself and the kids.

I signed across the paperwork and handed it to a delighted Hugo, who was already lighting up a fresh cigarette with an almost post-coital satisfaction. I rushed out of the car, feeling as though I had been unwittingly involved in an intimate moment between the machine and it's new owner. Waving him off, presumably with Ben's ghost still sobbing uncontrollably on the back seat of the car, I headed into the house feeling lighter than I had in weeks. Picking the post up off the floor, I skipped through the house into the kitchen and flipped on the kettle whilst idling wondering if it might be too early for a cheeky, albeit celebratory glass of wine.

Sifting through the envelopes, red lettering caught my eye and the light feeling dissipated slightly. I pulled the envelope out from the pile and saw that it was addressed to Ben. Pausing, I considered putting it in the bin, reasoning that if it was important enough to have red lettering it was unlikely to just go away that easily. In hindsight, I would say I knew what this was before I opened it, but it didn't help with the shock. I held the letter with shaking hands. It seems the executors of Ben's estate had somehow missed the car loan, which had now defaulted payment. The balance outstanding was just over ten thousand pounds. I'd just received thirteen thousand five hundred pounds for the car.

"Oh, for fuck's sake!" I screamed and shook my fist angrily into the sky. Two glasses of wine, a phone call to the loan company and the entire contents of the fridge later, my bank account boasted the princely balance of just over three thousand pounds.

"Well, that's better than nothing." Ben said with a wry smile as he appeared beside me.

"Yeah, but it's not nearly as nice as thirteen fecking grand." I spat back at him. I let out a huge, lung deflating sigh and calmed a little. "I was hoping to take the girls away in the Christmas holidays to get us away from the house."

"Sorry." Ben said still looking wretched.

"It's not your fault." I said taking a glug of wine and swallowing hard. When you've spent the past four weeks doing naught else but cry, you just get a bit bored of crying. I glared at the screen of my mobile, which was showing the now drastically diminished balance on my bank account, like some kind of evil traitor. "That's probably not going to last us a couple of months, especially with Christmas coming up."

I was brutally reminded of my need to find a job or at least some form of steady income, but it was not the thought of going to work every day that was making me sad. It was the loss of the freedom that I had enjoyed for most of my adult life. I was only twenty when I fell pregnant with Sophie. Ben was just finishing off his last year of university, so his parents were understandably less than thrilled. I had been working on the photo developing counter in Boots, which generally just involved placing "Over-exposed" stickers on pictures of genitals. I had never ceased to be amazed by the sheer balls of people who brought in their x-rated sex pictures for development in Boots. Although, that did tend to be more interesting than the endless twee family holiday photos and pictures of thumbs pressed against lenses. I recall once developing an entire reel of photographs of the inside of the camera lens cap. It was extremely hard not to laugh as seventy-year old Doris's smile of excitement turned to sour anger as she flipped through her photos at the counter. Whilst I was grateful that we live in more technologically advanced times, it did render ninety percent of the skills on my CV obsolete.

"Do you remember that little flat we had on Lenten street when Sophie was born?" I turned to Ben with a hint of a smile and he grinned back.

"You were convinced that place was haunted." He said, "Do you remember you kept saying things were being moved around because you couldn't find anything. Then I caught you one day trying to put the kettle in the fridge." We both laughed.

"Sleep deprivation can do terrible things to a woman. I'm still convinced it was haunted though. I used to hear weird noises all the time when you were at work. And it would suddenly get really cold and I'd feel like someone was watching us."

"Well, it was a fairly old building. It was probably just pipes or beams settling or something like that." He was being blithe but I'm sure he had had experiences in that little flat too. He was just refusing to admit it. An idea hit me.

"You should go back there and see if I was right." He looked less than enthusiastic.

"What? Just wonder in and say 'hello are there any ghosts here'? Don't be stupid!"

"Why not? No one will see you. Go on. Just stick your head through the door. Aren't you curious? I really want to know now. Oh, go on...for me?" I pouted a little and he rolled his eyes. Without another word his spirit faded into thin air.

While he was gone, I pulled out my laptop and fiddled about with websites and Facebook pages. By the time he had returned I had a fully formed business that just needed a name, but I slammed the laptop shut as I felt the tingle in the air and drop in temperature that indicated Ben was about to show up. When he did reappear, he looked pretty shaken up.

"Oh god, are you ok?" I asked. He looked longingly at my wine glass for a moment.

"I'm having a bad day." He said rubbing his face with his hand. I wanted to hug him more than anything, but worried that I would just fall through his spirit and land face first on the floor. The last thing the girls needed was to come home to me unconscious on the kitchen floor, reeking of wine. They'd suffered enough.

"Well...." I asked and I was smiling because I knew I'd been right.

"It's definitely haunted." He said lifting his eyebrows so high they were in danger of slipping off his forehead in true cartoon style. "She's mental...completely nuts." I grabbed my wine glass. If I'd had popcorn, I'd have been tucking in. This was going to be good. "It seems all I have to do is focus on somewhere and that's where I go. So, I show up in the living room of our old flat and there was no one there. Living or dead; looks like the place has been empty for a while. But then I get this feeling, like something is coming and it builds, and it builds and then this woman just comes tearing through the wall. She's screaming and grabbing at her clothes like she is on fire, but she looks angry, like, completely livid. As she came at me, I just backed off and we just passed through the wall and outside into the courtyard. I have no idea what she wanted or who she was, but I got the impression she wasn't happy about me being there...so I ran away. Well, floated away. I could really do with some wine right now." He licked his lips and eyeballed my glass again.

"That's terrifying. You look terrible. Are you ok?" I instinctively reached out to stroke his arm, but my hand just fell through like he was nothing but mist.

"Yeah, I'm fine. Gives me the shivers to think of you home alone with our baby daughter with that thing raging through the place." I shivered too. We only stayed at the flat for a year or so, but even still it was a horrific thought.

"So, we've established that you can see other

spirits, and you can communicate with them, if they aren't completely batshit crazy." His look was cynical, but he let me continue, "Could we say my idea might just work?" He sighed as hard as the disembodied spirit of a dead man could.

"What have you got in mind?" I immediately flipped open the laptop to show him our new business website and he squinted at the screen for several minutes. "You haven't got a name...you can't really be Tracey the Medium. It sounds ridiculous."

"I was thinking that. Tracey doesn't sound quite right. I could be Madame De La Fuente."

"Tracey De La Fuente?" he said with a grin, "Well, for a start Madame is French and De La Fuente sounds more Spanish. Not to mention the Tracey issue"

"Alright," I said, slightly irritated by his lack of support, "How about Senora Tatiana De La Feunte?" He laughed hard.

"Isn't Tatiana Russian?" I could tell he was really enjoying this and for a moment so was I.

"Tatiana Von Kanonononavichowitz?"

"Now that's just racist" he said, "How about just plain old Tracey Cringle?"

"Okay, I guess that will have to do." I smiled at him and he smiled back. His image was starting to fade slightly, reminding me that he couldn't stay forever.

"I'm sorry about your car by the way." I said and he shrugged.

"It's fine. I'm over it." He stepped forward and wrapped his translucent arms around me. I couldn't feel them but knowing they were there was enough. I turned my head so that my cheek was rested against his fading chest and we stood like that until he was completely gone.

7
(Before)

It was one of those family holidays that would one day be lost to legend, discussed often and for years to come. Ben had found the cottage online, a little brick farmhouse on the edge of Dartmoor, with a swimming pool, no less and only a short if hair-raising drive to the beach. Our first holiday to the West Country since the kids had been born and Ben's stellar career had given us the means to venture abroad once a year for a bit of sun and culture. That year, however, we had set our hearts on a new, bigger house in a nice part of town and all the while the mortgage adviser had toiled to get us what we needed for the move, we had committed to saving cash wherever we could. As far as Ben was concerned however, that didn't have to mean living like paupers and so the annual family holiday had only been scaled back ever so slightly. I suspected that when all was said and done, this jaunt would have cost us more than the normal trip to Turkey or Spain, but far be it from me to burst his bubble. He seemed to be comfortable with the lavish spend.

In truth we could have saved a lot of money by downgrading the cottage to something a bit smaller and without the swimming pool. Given the unpredictability of a British summertime, it was all a bit risky for my liking, but to my surprise the sun was beating down when we arrived at the cottage. The girls tore into the place, running up and down the hallways with heavy excited feet, choosing the rooms they wanted to stay in and eventually deciding to share a room with two adorable little single beds separated by a narrow bedside table. The room was tiny, but something about the cuteness was appealing to them so we let them get on with it. There were two other bedrooms for them to choose between if they wanted to. I didn't have to wash the sheets, so I was disinclined to give a shit.

We'd been at the cottage for less than an hour when the girls started to pester about getting in the pool. Realising that day might be the first and last sunny day, we hunted through the bags for the swimming costumes. Ben cracked open a beer and sat out on the terrace watching the girls fling themselves into the pool over and over again, while I sorted bags into rooms and unpacked the shopping we had picked up on the way. A woman's work is never done, or so they say and whilst I was content to know that my family were getting stuck in with the holiday festivities, it still would have been nice to have had a bit of help.

Once order had been achieved, I crept upstairs and struggled into my own bathing costume, figuring I would have some fun with the girls for a bit, but grabbing a paperback I'd packed for the holiday just in case I got the opportunity for a bit of leisure. I flip-flopped through the cottage and out onto the terrace where the girls were shouting and splashing. They were going through a real water-baby phase and begged every weekend to be taken to the local swimming pool.

It never got tired for them and I suspected that they would happily spend the entire holiday in a semi-aquatic state if we let them. They were at a beautiful age; utterly unencumbered by self -awareness. Life was all fun and games and laughing, with an occasional tantrum thrown in for balance, but they were almost always easy to mitigate. I desperately wished that I could stop time for them and selfishly keep them at this age forever. The teenage years were going to be a completely different ballgame and I was painfully aware of this inevitable fact.

"Mummy!" called out Sophie as she saw me walking towards the pool.

"Mummy, we're playing Shark-tag! Come on!" shouted Becky. I sat on the sun lounger beside Ben and placed my book on the floor. Fat chance of me getting a look at that then, I thought but I didn't really mind. They wouldn't be this age for long and I needed to make the most of every opportunity that I could.

"Ben, can you put some lotion on my back?" I asked and he looked across at me.

"What all of it?" he said with a smirk.

"That's the general idea." I gave him a withering look.

"Well, we are only here for a week, but if I start today, I might be finished by the time we head home." he sniggered. I laughed too because that was what we did. Sometimes when he was putting me down, he was actually quite funny. He could be fairly witty, and it was hard not to laugh, but that didn't change the fact that every comment he made was burrowing itself deep into my self-perspective. I had no objection to him being funny, but did I always have to be the butt of the joke?

When I'd first met Ben, I'd never wanted for a

boyfriend or attention from men. I was a lot slimmer then, but everyone puts on weight when they have children, don't they? The difference was, I'd been able to look in the mirror and feel happy with what I saw back then. Just the same old Tracey, with light blue eyes, long dark brown hair, a nose that was a tiny bit too big and a mouth that was a tiny bit too small but for the most part a nice enough face. I certainly hadn't had any complaints, that was for sure. Something changed after the girls had been born and from then I hadn't had the same time and energy to put into my appearance, but also I was horrifically tired most of the time which showed in the dark circles under my eyes, drooping face and increased propensity to stuff crumpets laden with butter and Nutella into my face. I could inhale a mars bar and did so most days just to keep myself going. I had gone up a single dress size and to begin with it hadn't bothered me too much but apparently, I wasn't seeing what Ben was seeing.

His comments started when Sophie was about six months old and he seemed to come to realisation that my figure was not just going to snap back to how it had been before. Perhaps he had thought that his barbed digs would incentivise me to get to the gym, but I simply didn't have the will or the energy to be exercising as well as raising a family. That really hadn't changed even when the girls were old enough to be looking at secondary schools. My philosophy remained that true love is blind, and he would love me through fat and thin, no matter what. I had managed to overlook his budding bald spot and hairy back, I'm sure he could forgive a few pounds.

The verbal attacks continued though, under the guise of humour and if I dared to confront him about his attitude, I was told to stop being so over sensitive and making a fuss. I would instantly feel bad, as though I had been unnecessarily harsh on him. Worst of all he would laugh at me and make me feel as though I was being stupid; how could I not see that he was only joking, silly woman! He had a way of making me feel ashamed and stupid but with a subtext of being unlovable.

As I waddled towards the pool, I could feel the disgust in his gaze on my pale, chubby body. That was the first time, in truth, it occurred to me that this was not what real love should feel like.

8

It couldn't be put off any longer. I had to visit my parents. I guess I should have felt more privileged that they had managed to fit me into their hectic schedule. Luckily for me they always left Friday mornings clear of bookings to prepare for a packed weekend. For a couple in their seventies they were ridiculously active, more out of professional pride and stubbornness than any need for financial gain. The weekend after the funeral they had been at Magifest UK, a not to be missed at any cost annual convention for all things magic. Surprising though it might seem, magic has always been a highly competitive field and mum and dad were battling to stay ahead of the competition, for their generation at least.

Mum answered the door after an age, resplendent in head to toe flannel with a perfectly made up face.

"Bit early for false eyelashes isn't it Mum?" I said. It was nine am. She dragged aggressively on her vape and her eyeballs bulged slightly reminding me of when you pet a cat's head too hard and its eyeballs protrude like they are going to pop out.

"It's never too early to look good love." She said

and stood aside to let me in. "Even at my age you have to stay ahead of the game. You should have seen some of the competition last week, I've got to keep up standards or I might lose my man." She realised too late the insensitivity of her comment and had the modesty to look mildly apologetic, "You know what I mean." She said.

I followed her into the kitchen at the back of the palatial bungalow they bought in the early nineties after Immy and I had left home. Dad had received a large compensation pay-out from the Fire Service after an accident that had left him with a buggered back and he had immediately invested in bricks and mortar and followed his dream to become a full-time magician. To our surprise and mild horror, he had been really rather good and quickly established an extremely successful business.

My towering bulk of a father was stood leaning against the kitchen counter and as I entered the room, he spread his arms wide. I snuggled into him. Nothing ever felt like home quite like a hug from Dad. For a brief moment I felt like a child, safe and happy and without all the worries that plagued me to the front door. I felt him kiss the top of my head, which barely reached his shoulders. We stood like that for several minutes, while mum flitted around flipping on the kettle and thumping mugs down on the countertop for the tea.

"You alright sweet-pea?" Dad asked and I nodded my head against his chest as I tried not to cry. It had been a rough week and I could just about hold it together until someone asked how I was, then somehow, I just wanted to unravel a bit at the edges. I could have told them about Ben and the car and the loan, but in that moment, I just wanted to talk about nothing important and pretend all the other stuff wasn't real.

"I'm fine Dad. How did the convention go?" I felt him stiffen in my arms.

"That fricking Balthezar, thieving bastard has been stealing my tricks again." Balthezar the Unbelievable, Prince of the Unknown (not his real name) has been Dad's rival in magic for his nearly two decades in the business. Balthezar, whose real name was Dave, still referred to my Dad as an "upstart" and "newcomer". I liked to think that their encounters at the MagiFest convention were not unlike the showdown in West Side Story, with rival gangs crowding around the two ringleaders chewing gum and clicking fingers in a threatening manner.

"Pete! Language!" Mum snapped.

"Thieving bastard!" Dad muttered again but was swiftly silenced by a single look from mum. I took a steaming cup of tea from her and we sat around the kitchen table. Mum and Dad sat opposite me, scrutinising me, clearly not convinced by my act of being "fine".

"How are my gorgeous granddaughters then?" Dad finally said.

"They seem to be doing okay." I said. I genuinely couldn't tell if they were truly coping extraordinarily well or if they were in fact just very good at putting on an act to make me feel better. I was at a loss as to how to tell the difference and even if it was the latter, what was I supposed to do? I considered, once again, telling them that I had seen their father's ghost, but I could only assume they would end up feeling the same pressing anxiety of being constantly watched that I had.

We were all concerned about the girls and the silence that fell over the room confirmed that. Mum stared into her tea while puffing away, billowing out cinnamon scented mist into the air. Dad watched a knot in the wood of the table intently, digging at it with a fingernail. None of us had any experience guiding children through a bereavement, let alone the death of their own father and I could sense that we were all feeling a bit inadequate. The school had contacted me to try and arrange counselling for them, but I just wasn't sure. I mentally added this to the list of things I needed to talk to Ben about along with how to bleed the radiators, where he had hidden the key to the garage, and I kept forgetting to ask again about the girl with no eyes.

I sighed heavily and my mother's eyes flickered with agitation.

"Come on now, no need to be so defeated. That won't get you anywhere." Her voice was stern, and my own irritation grew. She was, it seemed, incapable of feeling any kind of sympathy for me. The fuss she had made before the funeral had not been forgotten. Apparently, the date had been too close to the Magifest and they would have to re-book hotel rooms and change plans and so forth. "Oh, I'll contact Ben in the afterlife and let him know it's not a convenient time for him to drop dead, shall I?" I'd said at the time. Far from shutting her up, it had prompted an angry tirade from my mother. I recall being told I had a bad attitude, a familiar theme that had been going on since I had been a teenager, perhaps before. Just what you need to hear when you've just been widowed. My relationship with my mother was brittle at the best of times. If it hadn't been for my father, always the mediator, I suspect we would have stopped talking to one another a long time ago. It was for his sake and because I was there to ask a favour, that I swallowed down my bile and let the comment wash over me. Instead I focused on my Dad's face which was pained. He looked like he might be holding his breath, anticipating all-out war. I took a sip of my tea and mentally counted to ten.

"I was wondering if I could ask a favour." I said keeping my voice level. My mother's eyebrows (not the real ones which hadn't been seen since 1995, the ones she painted on) leapt up.

"Go for it pickle." said Dad, attempting to ignore my mother who was bristling beside him.

"I was wondering if you could come over one night and keep an eye on the girls so I can pop out."

"To do what?" Mum had barely let me finish.

"To be honest, I just need to get out of the house and do something for me for once." I met her eyes. "I was thinking about going to the cinema." I loved films. I always had. There was a small independent cinema in Alton that I had been known to frequent on pretty much a weekly basis. They ran black and white classics, Eighties Horror festivals and live shows of the ballet and west end theatre shows. This had been my only real indulgence for the past few years, Thursday evenings spent glued to the screen, huddled up on the back row scoffing popcorn and disappearing off to a make-believe land. Okay so it smelt a bit funny and was positively arctic from October right through to May, but it was my halcyon and there was nowhere I would rather be.

I saw my father start to agree, but Mum jumped straight in before he had the chance to utter a single word.

"Shouldn't you be out looking for a job? Immy was saying the other day things are a bit tight." It was said in a harsh, accusatory tone and I cursed my sister for telling Mum about our precarious finances. I was fairly sure it would have been coaxed out of her involuntarily though, so I decided not to hold it against her.

"I am looking for a job Mum," I said trying to stay calm, "and it is proving a struggle. I don't have much to offer, but I do have an opportunity I'm working on at the moment. I don't want to say too much right now in case it doesn't work out, but I'm pretty confident we will be fine."

"Well done love," Dad said and reached out to give my hand a squeeze, a gesture which I knew meant "If you get really stuck, I will help out, just don't tell mum." I beamed a smile of gratitude at him. I knew I could rely on his support and they were not short of a bob or two, but I needed to be able to do this for myself. I couldn't stand the idea of constantly putting on my parents to provide hand-outs. By the look on my mother's face, she felt precisely the same.

"If Ben had properly provided for his family, you wouldn't need to though would you?" She was clearly in a spiteful mood today and I decided I needed to get myself out of there as soon as I could before it really kicked off. But first I needed their help with this one small thing. I needed to get to that cinema.

"Hindsight is a wonderful thing." I said as righteously as I could muster. I sensed that Mum didn't quite get the sarcastic undertones and she nodded as if to acknowledge she had won this battle.

"So, if you're not busy Monday evening, would you mind popping over to watch the girls for me?" I addressed the question to Dad rather than Mum, even though I knew he would never agree unless she did. Right on cue, he looked to her for an answer.

"I don't see why you can't take them with you?" Mum said sipping her tea and eyeballing me suspiciously.

"I just need some time to myself. It's been a rough few weeks." I said miserably, sensing this was not going to end well. "I guess it doesn't matter. I just thought I would ask. Thanks anyway." I rose from my chair and drank the final dredges of my tea. Dad started to protest. "It's fine honestly. Thanks for the tea." I said with a tight smile and I made my way into the hallway. Mum just shrugged but Dad followed me out to the front door. He grabbed me for one more rib cracking hug and whispered into my ear.

"Let me have a word with your Mum. I'll see what I can do." he said, and I hugged him a bit tighter.

"Thanks Dad." I said, feeling no better for the sliver of a chance I might get what I need.

9

Back home I checked my emails. I was finding the business of being a psychic medium and paranormal investigator infuriating slow. So far, the only contact I had had was from advertising executives trying to sell me a hideously expensive premium space on their web listings and a rather plucky chap called Simon from China offering to redesign my website for me. Where did these people even come from and how did they find me so quickly, I pondered as I balanced my laptop on the edge of the sofa, my lap having been colonised by Norbert my ancient and somewhat judgmental tabby cat. He was sticking to me like glue, the frequent appearances of Ben having shattered his last nerves. Poor old boy was only just recovering from Bonfire night too, although, at the ripe old age of fourteen I had rather expected that this would have been his last Bonfire night. Contrary to my expectations, he soldiered on just getting grumpier and more tatty with each year. I tickled him behind the ear to show him that I still loved him, and he looked up to me giving me a full facial blast of fish flavoured cat breath.

      I decided to log onto Facebook, which I had been fastidiously avoiding since Ben died. There's nothing like someone dying in their prime to bring out the worst in some people. Of course, most of my friends had been supportive in a manner befitting the nature of our relationship prior to my husband passing away. Others it seemed appeared to be shifting closer, like hideous vultures picking at the carrion of my misfortune. One, an old school friend called Kirsty, had shown up at the house just two days after Ben had died, seemingly alerted to the tragedy by a post my sister had made on my profile to let people know what was going on and asking for love and support at a difficult time. Given that I hadn't seen Kirsty in the flesh since our last day at secondary school, I could be forgiven for not recognising her when she first pitched up on my doorstep, with a potted Peace Lily. She had thrust me into her substantial bosom and then invited herself in, making us both a fortifying cup of tea. She'd stayed for two whole hours and it had taken the appearance of my mother, who was standing for none of that nonsense to scare her off. Within days she was posting about her own grief on my behalf all over Facebook and sharing twee life-affirming messages on my wall. At the funeral, she even had the brass to strategically position herself in the pew behind me, reaching forward to squeeze my shoulder periodically. It took all my inner strength not to turn around and shout at her to fuck off.

The Facebook business page for my new venture was linked to my personal profile and so logging in was inevitable to check in on business and see if I had any new messages. I managed to ignore the twenty or so message notifications and dove straight onto the business page. Squeaking with surprise, I clicked on the inbox to open the one shiny new message that had arrived. A woman called Cheryl appeared to have sent me her entire life story. I speed read through, eager to see if there was a point, but a few words sprung out and stopped me in my tracks. I went back to read the whole thing more thoroughly, giving it the attention it deserved.

Cheryl was a twenty-two year-old apprentice hairdresser, Alton born and bred. She explained she had only just started her training, despite wanting to be a hairdresser since she was a toddler when her dad gave her one of those styling head toys (apparently her older brother gave it a grade two not long after, but this didn't stop her dreaming). Even though I had never met her and in spite of her long and rambling message, I quickly warmed to this young woman. She went on to tell me that her mother had been physically abusive for as long as she could remember, before she was eventually taken into care at the age of ten. Her adult life hadn't been much better, and she had suffered years of severe, debilitating anxiety and agoraphobia that left her completely housebound for over a year and a half. My heart wrenched for her and I was desperate to understand how she thought I could help. At the end of the message she explained that she had recently met a man she thought she liked and could possibly trust, and she was asking if I could give her a reading to help her decide what to do.

I sat back in the chair and thought. Suddenly this all seemed so brutally real and foolhardy. How could I possibly give direction to such a damaged girl, who needed proper help and support? I started to draft a response to explain that I was afraid I couldn't help because...because...I struggled. What if she decided to go see someone else and they were a complete charlatan like me? A rush of maternal defensiveness stopped me in my tracks, and it seemed as if it might be my duty to help her somehow. Frustrated by my impotence, I shouted out Ben's name into the empty house, with no idea if it really was that easy to summon the dead. I waited a second or two in silence and shouted his name again, trying to sound as impatient as I felt.

"I really need you, are you there?" I called out, hoping the neighbours couldn't hear me through the shared wall. To my surprise he did appear, perched on the end of the sofa, one eyebrow raised. Norbert scarpered sharpish, the cat-flap banging in his haste to escape.

"Need me, eh?" he winked, and I rolled my eyes.

"Not like that." He looked a little disappointed but I'm not sure how he thought he could have possibly helped me without a physical body. "I've had this message. Take a look." Ben disappeared and then reappeared instantly beside me. He started to read the message and then sighed impatiently. "Properly please." I said, eliciting another loud sigh. It took him a while to read through and I started to worry that we wouldn't have enough time before he had to go again. Eventually, he stopped reading and looked at me.

"Hmmn." I could sense his reticence, but I'd been reading through the message again as he was reading and I was even more certain that we needed to help this girl, if we could.

"We need to help her." I said.

"How?"

"I don't know." I was rather hoping he would have some suggestions, but his brow was knitted, and we sat in contemplative silence. "Could you contact some of her deceased relatives somehow? Perhaps they could help? I guess the rest is just common sense. I'll listen to what she has to say about her new fella and I'll give her advice the same as I would any of my friends if they were in the same position."

"And you would be comfortable charging her money for this?" he wasn't using a challenging tone. I guessed he could sense my own hesitation.

"No." I said straight away, "I wouldn't be happy doing that. I think I would tell her the first session is a freebie and if it went well, I guess we could just cross that bridge when we come to it. Do you think you could go and check out this new guy she's thinking of seeing?"

"Err...I really don't know Trace."

"Please?" Regardless of whether or not we went ahead with the reading, I wanted to know this new man was going to be right for Cheryl. Poor girl had been through enough, she could do without any dickheads messing her around. Ben shrugged.

"I'll try." I smiled gratefully at him.

"Thanks honey." Without thinking I reached across to hold his hand, but my hand landed on the empty couch and we shared an amused look. "Oh! Before I forget again, did you ever find out who the girl with the missing eyes was?" He shook his head.

"I don't know everything, you know." Thank god for that, I thought. "I can't sense anyone here right now, if that's any help. Are you sure it wasn't a dream?"

"It felt pretty real." I said thoughtfully, "But then I was pretty tired so maybe. I guess it's a good thing if I can see ghosts without your help though. For our new venture."

"How about you go check out that crazy mess in our old flat and find out for sure?" he grinned.

"How about no..." I said. Not a bloody chance. There were some things I wasn't ready for.

Ben lingered far longer than he had since he had started appearing and we sat side by side, like old times and talked. Mundane stuff, important house stuff, a bit of gossip, all the while tiptoeing around the topic of our girls. I could tell he wasn't ready to have that conversation with me just yet. It was too soon and too raw. The thought of being separated from my daughters would be enough to drive me to the brink of insanity, so I couldn't imagine what he was going through. I only hoped that being able to see them and be close to them was somehow providing a little comfort to him. He disappeared shortly before they were due home from school. Having sent a response across to Cheryl, I slipped the laptop onto the floor and sat back into the chair, staring into space, deep in thought. Within seconds, I felt my eyelids droop and the inevitable rush of exhaustion, only to be woken what seemed like minutes later by a noise outside the window.

Blearily, I peeled my eyes open and turned to the pane, where a grotesque face was gurning back at me. I screamed and hurled myself off the sofa.

10

"I'm sorry Mrs Cringle" blurted Callum at me as I lay on the floor. He appeared in the living room moments later, having been let in by Sophie. His cheeks were burning red with embarrassment and yet he still wore the cheekiest of grins.

"Idiot," I muttered under my breath and held out my hand for him to help me up. Callum had been Sophie's best friend since infant's school. Incorrigibly goofy, but equally caring and kind, he had been rock-solid for her. His mother, Claire, and I were secretly hoping they ended up getting married one day, to the point discussions regarding hats and venues had been had. He was a sweet lad and she could do so, so much worse, but as Ben always reminded me, I had to try not to interfere and just let the kids get on with it. Easier said than done.

Sophie appeared at the door to the living room carrying a porcelain casserole dish.

"Callum's mum made us a lasagne." She said. Becky's head appeared around the door.

"Oh, wow that looks good." She said and it really did. Claire was the most incredible cook and had been sending me regular food parcels over the past few weeks, which was the only reason we hadn't all perished from malnutrition. I had just been flinging horrific freezer food into the oven in the interim and hoping for the best. Sophie's efforts had kept us topped up, between freezer food junk and filthy takeaways, but even still, it was a miracle that we had all survived.

Once the oven was on and the precious lasagne smell was wafting through the house, I started to feel a tiny bit like a normal functioning adult, which came as some surprise. Laughter drifted down the stairs from Sophie's room where her and Callum were "doing their homework" and loud, thumping music came from Becky's room where she was no doubt curled up on her bed with her mobile glued to her face, eyeballs darting back and forth over the screen and thumbs working overtime to tap out messages. I stood in the kitchen, leaning against the breakfast bar, feeling an overwhelming sense of normality and calm, for which I was disproportionately grateful. I closed my eyes for a moment to enjoy the bustle and noise and smell and warmth of my home. When I reopened them, I found Ben stood the other side of the breakfast bar watching me, smiling.

"Can I help you?" I said with the hint of a smile.

"Yes, you can actually," he said, "I'm looking for Tatiana Von Vonkanonononavichowitz. Do you know where I might find her?" He grinned.

"Well remembered!" I laughed, hoping no-one upstairs could hear me and think I was talking to myself. Presumably they would not be able to hear Ben's side of the conversation, but if they heard me say his name, they could well assume I'd finally lost all of my remaining marbles. My mobile vibrated on the side and I grabbed it, angling the screen towards me. I could feel

Ben's ghostly stare on my face and hoped I wasn't turning red. There was an email from Cheryl and curiosity overtook my panic.

"It's from Cheryl," I said my eyes glued to the phone, "She can do Monday afternoon." I was a little surprised and suddenly quite nervous.

"It's going to be fine." He always was good at picking up on how I was feeling.

"Can you tell that because you can see into the future or are you just saying it to make me feel better?" I asked earnestly.

"I've already said, I can't see into the future." he sounded impatient now, "But I'm not just saying it to make you feel better either. I've managed to track down some of Cheryl's relatives on the other side and they have agreed to help out at the reading."

"Thank fuck for that." I said.

"That fuck for what?" said Becky who had appeared in the kitchen doorway, eyes still cast down on her phone. She glanced up and cast her gaze suspiciously around the room.

"I managed to get up a level...on Candy Crush...I've been stuck on that level for ages." I gestured at my phone on the worktop and Becky rolled her eyes theatrically. "Anyway, language young lady!"

"No offence Mum, but are you not getting a little old for Candy Crush?" I was affronted and so I gasped, clasping a hand to my chest.

"How very dare you!" I said. Ben was watching the exchange, with a wide smile. I wished I could tell Becky, but she already thought I was old. She didn't need to think I was old and mad. "Anyway, how was school sweet-pea?" She harrumphed in response which I took to mean something along the lines of "okay".

"I need you to put some more cash on my canteen account..."

"Please..." said Ben out of habit, to remind her of her manners.

"Please." added Becky. Ben and I look at each other in alarm. Her face is still glued to the screen of her mobile. I widened my eyes at Ben, and he shrugged.

"Yeah, I'll do it now." I said picking up my phone and logging into the school account on my phone, flashing looks at Ben as I did so. He stood right next to her, at first waving his hands in front of her face. She didn't flinch. The next time I looked up he was trying to blow across her face. Her fringe shifted a little and she wrinkled her nose, batting away the hair with her hand. Seconds later I looked up to see my late husband's ghost doing a full hoedown dance beside her. I guffawed involuntarily and Becky looked up. I held up the phone in my hand.

"Funny meme on Facebook." I said and she rolled her eyes again.

"You are also too old for memes," she said standing up and walking to the door. She peeled her gaze away from the mobile to stare me directly in the eye, "And you are most certainly too old for Facebook." She turned on her heel and skulked off to the living room. I turned to look at my deceased husband.

"She gets her attitude from you, you know." I whispered. Ben was still looking after her. He turned to me after a while.

"Do you think she heard me? It was just coincidence wasn't it?" I shook my head.

"I think she heard your voice in her head, because you've spent her entire life reminding her to say please. That's your legacy. Well part of it anyway."

His face was hard to read, but I sensed a mixture of pride and sadness.

"So, Cheryl..." I prompted him. It was hard to see him like that.

"Oh yeah, Cheryl. I've found a great uncle who died when she was a little girl, but he's been keeping a close eye on her. He's a bit creepy if I'm honest, but beggars can't be choosers. I also have her Nan on her Mum's side and get this...I've got her Mum. And they are all willing to come to the reading."

"Her Mum?" I was shocked. I'd expected the relationship to be too strained for her to come forward. My sense of foreboding rushed back like a relentless tide. This was not necessarily good news and certainly complicated things. "She didn't mention that her mum was dead."

"I don't think they have had any contact since Cheryl was taken into care, from what I can tell. She was dead keen ('scuse the pun) to come forward and communicate with her. Said she'd missed her little girl so much, yadda yadda... she went on about it for ages."

"Bit weird." I was getting a bad feeling, but we had no choice. It was crucial to get as much back up as possible, so it was probably best to just go with it and hope for the best. "Did you have any joy tracking down the boyfriend?"

"Yes. He seems okay. Bit nerdy and, if you want my honest opinion, wet behind the ears, but otherwise seems ok. Hard to tell if he is a serial killer at this early stage but I'll keep sneaking back over the weekend to see if I can catch him out."

"Great, I need you to try and get some information that I can use in the reading. Like what he looks like, anything she would know about him that wouldn't be obvious...you know what I mean."

"Like the fact he likes to wear women's underwear?" He said.

"No way!" I gasped.

"He doesn't, I'm just saying, stuff like that?" I shot him a withering look.

"Maybe not stuff precisely like that. Like his favourite tv show or any little habits that he has." Ben nodded enthusiastically.

"Ok, I'm on it." I trusted him to get the job done, but at the same time worried he might not have fully understood the brief. There was nothing for it now though. I was entirely at the mercy of my dead husband to pull this off.

11

I was pacing the hallway nervously when Cheryl tapped on the front door. She didn't look like I expected she would. Strawberry blonde curls tumbled down her shoulders, framing an immaculately made up face. Her soft round cheeks crinkled into delightful dimples as she smiled at me shyly. She waved her hand at me, the sleeves of her jumper pulled down over her hands so only the tips of her manicured fingers were showing.

"Cheryl?" I said, trying out my professional 'I completely know what I'm doing' voice. She nodded, "Come on in." I stepped aside to let her through and between us we filled my little hallway. I lead her through into the kitchen and then into the conservatory, where I had set up a small table and two chairs facing each other. I had procrastinated for an extraordinarily long time over whether to invest in a crystal ball for the centre of the table, but I eventually decided that it would come across as disingenuous. Besides, what if she had asked me to use the damn thing? I had, however invested in a pack of tarot cards; a bargain at £9.99 from Waterstones. I'd spent most of the weekend, desperately attempting to remember the meanings of each of the cards before deciding I would just wing it and keep it vague. With any luck Ben would be able to point me in the right direction if I got really stuck.

"Please take a seat," I said pointing to one of the wooden fold-out chairs I had stolen from the garden. As we both sat, I immediately regretted my choice of seating. We both spilled out the sides of the chairs and shifted uncomfortably. Cheryl was good tempered about it, despite saying nothing she beamed at me throughout, rolling up one of her sleeves to reveal a twenty-pound note clutched in her hand. She held it out to me.

"No really," I said, "No fee for the first meeting. We need an opportunity to connect and err...ensure that there is a strong enough connection with the other side." I said as I looked around desperately. My friends from the afterlife hadn't actually showed up so I was in a little bit of a panic.

"Oh, are you sure?" she asked. Her brow was furrowed, and I could tell she wasn't comfortable with a freebie.

"Honestly, I am absolutely sure." I gently pushed her hand back. "Now, what I would like to do, is for you to lay your hands, palm up on the table. I will place my hands on top of yours and we will invite the spirits to step forward." I delivered this preamble with such authority you would not have thought I pulled together this technique from binge watching YouTube videos all evening. She smiled again and it struck me she really was a spectacularly pretty young woman, but utterly self-conscious in a way that was adorable, which made me all the more protective of her. We sat with our hands touching for several moments and I closed my eyes, face cast down at my lap. I could feel her watching me intently, full of eager anticipation. Mentally I was screaming out to Ben to hurry the hell up. As I was just starting to break out in a cold sweat, I felt the temperature drop almost imperceptibly. I sensed Cheryl grow uneasy and looked up to see her wide-eyed gazing about the little room. I could sense that there was someone to my left and I knew intuitively that it was not Ben. There was no form of a person there, but I could sense something was in the room with us.

"So," I turned to Cheryl and she snapped her attention back to me, a somewhat more nervous smile on her face, "did you have any specific questions for me today?"

"Umm..." she chewed on her sleeve a little, "I think, yeah, I think I just want to know about this guy I've met. Jack. I met him at the book shop, you know the little second hand one near the train station?" she waits for me to nod, "I like it in there because it's so cramped with shelves and books and stuff and it just makes me feel like I'm in there all on my own. Anyway, I was in there looking for a new book, I love those detective novels, you know like the ones about the Woman Detective Agency?" she looked to me for reassurance again and I was seized by a panic that she wouldn't actually stop talking. I nodded even though I had no idea what she was talking about. "I've read most of them and I was looking to see if I could find something like that but a bit different. Jack was in there at the same time looking for the same thing and he was just like, wow, you're well beautiful and I was like, oh my god he's so cute. I've never spoken to a guy I didn't know like that before. So, he gives me his number and now we've met for three dates." She didn't actually stop talking, but to my immense relief Ben started to appear in the corner of the room midway through her speech, his opaque shape giving me an unmistakable double thumbs up. "We went to Costa twice and then the cinema to watch the new Avengers film, have you seen it?" I shook my head no, I had thought it was a children's film. She was about to re-launch the conversation when I held up my hand to stop her.

"Don't give me too much information, not just yet." I said, even though she already had. To my left I could make out two shadowy forms slowly materialising, in addition to the presence which it seemed was still not ready to reveal itself. "Now, I'm sensing that there are three spirits present with us today, they are just making themselves known to my spirit guide." Ben sat a little taller, obviously chuffed with his new accolade. Beside him I could make out an old man, so painfully thin the bones cut deep ridges in his papery skin. He was the deep brown tone of an ancient paperback. Beside him was a hefty, middle-aged lady with a grey bubble perm. They were having a heated argument. I looked to Ben who shrugged.

"I present you with Great Uncle Gordon and Great Nanna Shirley. Good luck." Said Ben and he sat back with obvious relish.

"No, I'm telling you, she was a complete slaaaaag!" shouted Great Nanna Shirley as I tried to control the look on my face for Cheryl's benefit. "Oh, look Gordo, look at our little Cheryl."

"Not so little anymore" chuckled Gordon. I turned to Cheryl.

"I'm getting an older gentlemen. He knew you when you were much younger." Cheryl's eyes were wide with wonder and she scooted right forward onto the edge of her creaking seat.

"Yeah, right little firecracker she was too." He said. I tried to control my gag reflex.

"Now I feel this older gentleman is a generation moved back and err...to the side, so this would mean a great uncle perhaps?" Cheryl's eyebrows shot up and I had to hold up a hand to stop her shouting out names. This was where I needed to prove my worth. "I'm getting a name through..." dramatic pause, "It's a G name I think..."

"Gordon." Said Gordon, Shirley and Ben in unison.

"It sounds like a Go... Gor...umm...Gor..." I closed my eyes to concentrate and creased my brow in mock concentration.

"Gordon. It's Gordon." Shouted Gordon, "She's a bit fick your missus ain't she." He said to Ben, who shrugged and tried to sink in against the wall.

"Gor...Gord...ok my love I think I've got it." The spirits look bemused at my performance. "Do you have a Great Uncle called Gordon spirit side?" I asked.

"Yes!" screamed Cheryl and she jumped up in her seat.

"Okay. I have your Great Uncle here with us today and also there are two other spirits." I looked to Ben, who was frowning.

"Two?" he mouthed.

"The first, is an older lady, although I don't think she was that old when she passed." I said and Shirley patted her bubble perm triumphantly. Gordon laughed like it was the funniest joke he had ever heard, and Shirley shot him a foul look.

"I'm her mother's mother. My name is Shirley dear." She reached out a ghostly hand to pat my knee.

"There is a maternal link with this lady, so that would be on your mother's side." I've perfected my patter, binge watching Psychic Suze on the TV. "With this lady I'm getting an S name, it's a Sh noise.

"Shirley dear, like I just said" Shirley looked to Ben, "Fucking thick as pig shite."

"Like Sharon...or maybe Shirley. No, it's definitely Shirley. Does that make sense to you?" I asked Cheryl who is almost dumbstruck with wonder. Nailed it.

"My Great Nanna was called Shirley." She gasped. Yeah that's what I just said, I thought, but I just nodded sagely.

"Let me see if she has a message for you." I said closing my eyes and praying that the ghost of Great Nanna Shirley got the message. After a few moments of silence, I cracked open one eye to find everyone in the room was looking at me in stunned curiosity. "About your new relationship." I said a little louder. Silence. "I will see...if your Great Grandmother Shirley...has a message for you...about your new relationship with Jack." I looked to Shirley and she jumped a little as the penny dropped.

"Oh, right you're asking me. Oh right. Well, I guess he's ok isn't he. Nice enough chap. Not too bright mind. Never going to set the world on fire, sadly. But then, bless her, probably the best our girl can hope for. Mind she's a pretty one, but not all that clever herself you know." She looked at me enthusiastically to check if she's done good and I sighed heavily.

"Okay Cheryl, so your Great Nanna is telling me." I was interrupted by Gordon as I tried to interpret what I'd been told into something more tactful.

"He's a big Poof!" shouted Great Uncle Gordon,

"Not in the bumming lads kind of way, you understand." Ben sniggered. "No lad I know worth 'is salt sits around playing those bleedin' daft wizard and warlock games. He should be out drinking ale and smoking. Like a real man!" He looked indignant.

"Your Great Nanna is telling me that she likes him. He is a nice type. Steady and dependable. She thinks you could be happy together." Shirley looked confused.

"I didn't!" she mumbled.

"Your Great Uncle has mentioned that Jack enjoys Board games, the roleplay ones?" I said. Cheryl gasped.

"He does!" she whispered reverently.

"Well your Uncle is of a very different generation," I smiled kindly and chuckled slightly, "It's not the kind of thing he would have done in his time. But he too has ...err...a fondness...of sorts, for Jack." It was worth the little white lie, as relief swept Cheryl's face and she clasped her hands to her chest.

"I knew he was the one." She said and a single tear slipped down her cheek.

"Listen, Cheryl," I said reaching across the table to take her hands in mine, "You don't need anyone to tell you how you feel about this guy. If it feels right to you, just take it nice and slow and I know that you will be absolutely fine."

"Oh, will she now?" A cold voice cut through room and everyone, including the unliving contingent of the room, turned to a female figure that had appeared. The woman was small and thin, with blond hair scraped back severely from her forehead. Her face was pinched up, like she had pure spite rippling underneath her skin. The temperature in the room dropped several degrees rapidly and I felt Cheryl's hands tremble in mine. I knew instantly who this was and although Cheryl couldn't see the tiny apparition in the corner, I sensed she knew too.

"Cheryl has your mother passed?" I asked. She nodded dumbly.

"Please tell me she's not here..." Her voice was a childlike whisper. I turned to her.

"I'm sorry, she is here, but she cannot hurt you now." Before I could even finish the sentence, the spirit howled into the room. I looked to Ben in panic and he looked back equally panicked. The tablecloth on the flimsy table flapped against our legs as her rage swirled around the room. I held Cheryl's hand tighter and looked into her eyes. "Did you hear me Cheryl? She cannot hurt you now. You have nothing to be afraid of." I was amazed by how confident I sounded but didn't feel. The poor girl was sobbing but attempted a nod at me. The tarot cards were caught up in the turmoil and drifted off the table, swirling around the room like we were in the eye of a storm. "Cheryl, look at me." I said firmly. Her eyes were wide with fright and tears tumbled down her cheeks, but she nodded again, this time it was more convincing. "You need to tell your mother. She cannot hurt you anymore."

"You can't hurt me anymore." Cheryl whispered and I felt the anger in the spirit swell, filling all the space in the room.

"Louder" I shouted. "Tell her she cannot hurt you anymore!"

"You cannot hurt me anymore." She said timidly, then "Mother! You cannot hurt me anymore!" she shouted into the room with sudden ferocity.

"Oh really!" the spirit of her mother sneered. A small porcelain figurine of a cat, which had been sat on my dining room sideboard quivered and then slowly rose into the air.

"What is with you lot and hurling about my porcelain!" I shouted, exasperated. "Cheryl look out!"

Before she could get out of the way, the figurine shot across the room, hitting Cheryl square between the eyes. She went cross-eyed for a moment and then her chair fell backwards, landing on the floor with a thump.

"Norma Deborah Hayward!" Great Nanna Shirley rose up, red face livid. "What the hell do you think you are doing young lady." The room stopped swirling instantly, the ghost of Cheryl's mother suddenly looked half the size, staring down at her feet. Shirley reached back her hand, wide and far before administering the most violent thick ear I had ever seen in my life, so much so it seemed to knock Cheryl's mother back into the afterlife.

"I'm sorry about this dear," Shirley said to me, as an ethereal door seemed to open in the centre of the room, and she shuffled towards it. She looked down at Cheryl lying unconscious on the floor, "Sweet girl. She'll be fine."

Great Uncle Gordon stood and plucked a flat cap out of thin air, slapping it onto his bald head. He simply shrugged and then followed Shirley through the door which promptly shut after them and disappeared.

Ben and I looked at each other, both mirroring stark shock. We stood in unison and walked over to where Cheryl was still motionless on the floor.

"Well...shit." said Ben. "That didn't go well." I'd almost forgotten his propensity for pointing out the bloody   obvious.

12

Ben found me several hours later, lying on the couch with a cold flannel on my face. I'd only been back ten minutes from dropping Cheryl at A&E. She'd insisted I didn't wait with her. It had taken several minutes to bring her round and check for concussion, another thirty minutes to stop the uncontrollable sobbing and administer ice to the large red dent in her face and then another half an hour to attempt to talk her down from the horrific experience that was her first reading with me on, whilst our way to the hospital. I felt dreadful. By the time we parted, she had regained some composure, having allowed me to convince her not to let this morning's events ruin all of her progress. Being the font of kindness that she was Cheryl was far from upset with me and actually thanked me for my help, which only served to make me feel even worse.

As soon as I had gotten home, I had inhaled half a packet of custard creams and literally crawled to the couch. I had sensed Ben's appearance and so had no need to remove the flannel from my face.

"Everything ok?" he asked, using the timid voice he had always reserved for when I might be angry or stressed. I just grunted. There were no words for what had happened that morning. Not one. "That was pretty intense. I wasn't really expecting that. Who knew, scummy people are still scummy in the afterlife?"

"They were completely vile." I whimpered. If he'd been alive, Ben might have stroked my forehead, but he wasn't so he just sat awkwardly on the other end of the sofa. "I'm never doing that again."

"Probably a good idea to stay away from readings like that. Too unpredictable." He said. I had been so optimistic about that first reading. My new venture was an opportunity to be earning a decent income from home, with the flexibility to be around for the girls and the possibility of actually helping people. But following that disastrous morning, I was a tenner down and I guessed about three weeks from destitution. I'd already put my new tarot cards on Ebay to lessen the blow. I had one bid for two pounds and thirty pence. I could have cried. In fact, I could have done more than cry, and for the first time in my life I was considering throwing myself off a bridge. I was glad that I had a flannel on my face so Ben couldn't see me welling up with frustration and self-pity.

"Don't cry Trace." I pulled the flannel of my face and hurled it in his direction. It sailed through his translucent face and landed against the wall with a wet thud.

"I don't know what to do." I said miserably.

"You need to check your emails." He sounded like he knew something I didn't.

"Why?" I struggled to sit up so I could get a proper look at his face.

"Just do it." He nodded his head in the direction of the laptop, charging on the sideboard. Wearily I stood, shuffled over the laptop wearing my blanket like a shroud, and shuffled back, hurling myself back onto the sofa into the corner nook which was my appointed spot. While it loaded, I looked at him, trying to scrutinise his face for clues. He definitely knew something.

There was a single email in my inbox. I didn't recognise the name but opened it anyway.

"How did you know about this?" I asked him.

"I've been visited." He said.

"Who by?" He shrugged again. I was starting to get irritated.

"I don't know. I was just told this was something you have to do." I turned back to the computer and read the email. It is from a woman called Erin. She explained that she and her husband had recently taken over the lease at The Crown Inn in town. They had spent some time refurbishing the pub and restaurant and had recently reopened, but they had to close again almost immediately. She was living in the staff quarters at the top of the hotel with her husband and daughter and there had been "strange occurrences". They'd already had several waiting staff walk out, refusing to even come back into the building to pick up their wages. She explained that they had sunk every last penny they have into this venture and they were terrified of losing everything. She asked if I could help her. My immediate thought was, no I can't.

"How can I do this? I can't even handle a simple reading!" I wailed at Ben. I desperately wanted to help, but that day I was convinced more than ever that this was not the right career path for me.

"Listen, you couldn't have helped what happened this morning. No-one could have predicted that evil witch would have showed up and I don't know what any other medium would have done about it either."

"No." I said slamming the laptop shut, "I'm not cut out for this and I am done with ghosts and the afterlife and any of that nonsense." The temperature in the room dropped. From the shocked look on Ben's face and the way he was looking around the room frantically, I could tell he didn't know what is going on either. The lights flickered on, then off, then buzzed frantically.

"She's not happy." Ben said and I shivered.

"Who?"

"The girl with no eyes..." he said and turned to me, "She's here." He pointed to the far corner of the dining room. A small black shape, a young girl, was turned to the wall hunched over as if crying into her hands. The sight of her filled me with terror.

"What does she want?" I whispered to Ben.

"She wants you to take on the case."

"I can't, I'm..." the lights flickered more violently, the temperature dropped again and the sound of the little girl's sobs filled the room. "I'm not the right person, I can't deal with stuff like this." Now the sobs sounded angry, bitter and the little shape in the corner of the room seemed to grow. I couldn't take my eyes off her, but I didn't want to see her little pale face, with the deep red gorges where her eyes should be.

"Trace please." Said Ben, his voice was quivering with fear. I'd never known him so scared.

"But what if I cock it up and make things worse?" The wailing intensified. The lightbulb above our heads buzzed and then smashed, littering us with glass. Ben turned to me, his eyes pleading.

"I had no idea LEDs could do that." He said,

then added "You've got to try."

"Ok, ok, I'll try. I promise I'll try, but I really don't think...". The sobbing stopped and the temperature in the room returned to normal. The room brightened and I realised how dark the room had become. I looked to the corner of the room where the little figure had stood, and it was empty.

I hadn't realised it was possible for a ghost to turn pale as if they had seen a ghost, until I saw the look on Ben's face. He fell back into the seat, then through the seat before pulling himself back in line with the edge of the couch. Being a ghost in a physical world was tricky logistically it seemed. I managed a weak smile, although his reaction had me seriously concerned. We had no idea what we were dealing with here and I hated the idea of that thing in the house with my girls.

"Who is she and why does she want me to do this job so bad?" I asked him.

"Honestly if I knew I would tell you Trace."

"Could it be her? Haunting the Crown, I mean?" he thought about it for a minute and then shook his head.

"That wouldn't make any sense. I don't think. Why would she want us there if it was her and why not just tell us what is going on?"

"Maybe it's a trap?" I said and we both shifted uneasily in our seats. "Either way, I think you need to get down there and check it out." I could tell he didn't savour the prospect. I wondered if he would try and put it off, like he did with upping the cover on his life insurance, not that I was still bitter about it. He was a master in the art of procrastination, but I needed to find a way to keep him occupied for the rest of the day. "Maybe get some rest and go there this evening to see if you can get a clue what's going on?" I suggested.

"Fine." He said and we sat in silence for a while. It might just have been paranoia but for a moment I was convinced that he had read my mind. His mood had shifted subtly. I had been married to this man for nearly fourteen years so I knew every nuance of his personality and I could tell he was brooding. Perhaps I should have told him where I was going that evening and just addressed the elephant in the room. Something told me, however, that he already knew.

A key clicked in the door and the sound of shuffling adolescents filled my hallway. Ben met my eyes and started to fade silently. I couldn't speak, so I just watched him go.

13
(Before)

A brief respite from motherhood was always welcome but never for too, too long, or I ended up feeling guilty. As I bustled through the door fully laden with shopping bags, mainly full of clothes for me, I found Ben and the girls sat cross legged on the carpet, in the lounge engaged in a lively debate over a game of monopoly. Having tired of the noise and palaver, Norbert the cat had wondered halfway across the board and stopped momentarily to lick his balls, whilst he had everyone's attention.

"Ah Christ! Can you fetch us an antibacterial wipe love?" shouted Ben and I dumped down my bags and rushed to the kitchen. Yes, it's nice to have a break, but it's always nicer to feel wanted. After Norbert had gotten bored and sulked off and the board has been wiped down, everyone's attention was instantly turned to the contents of my shopping bags.

"Oh no, it's all for me!" I said with a wicked grin. The girls groaned and Ben peeked into one of the bags.

"Err...I don't think this is your size dear." he said pulling out a pink fluffy jumper, which would undoubtedly fail to fit over my sizable bosom, but that was mostly because it was a children's size.

"Ah no, that is for Sophie." She jumped up with a squeal and held it up against herself. Before Becky could get a sulk on, I reached into another bag and pulled out a sweatshirt, covered in rips with the word Rebel printed on the front. Becky broke into a grin before she could gain control over her face and I passed her the jumper.

"Thanks Mum" she said admiring the logo at arm's length before pulling it on.

"And not forgetting the wonderful man that made all of this possible…" I reached into another bag and pulled out a handful of new tee-shirts and handed them to Ben. He pawed thorough each one to check it met his exacting standards before accepting the gift with equanimous gratitude and a little nod of the head. I grasped up the rest of the bags and dashed upstairs, yelling "And the rest is definitely for me." Next was the fun bit; trying everything on.

I had long coveted a certain style requiring knee length boots combined with a little A-line skirt and thick black tights; just right for the Autumn. I had always assumed this style wasn't for me on account of my shot-putter's calves which were a little beyond chunky. Recently, however, a shop for more robust ladies (such as myself) had opened in the shopping centre in Basingstoke and they had stocked knee length boots in a wider fitting. It had been a bit of a faff to find the right sizing for me and the shop assistant had assured me that I looked really great in my new boots before I parted with the best part of a hundred quid, but they tend to do that don't they. I surveyed my new ensemble in the mirrored door of our built-in wardrobe, something I generally was reluctant to do if I could possibly avoid it, and I was surprised how happy I was with how I looked.

I had practically skipped down the stairs to show my family my new outfit. I'd pranced up and down the lounge once I'd torn their attention from their game, posing in an exaggerated catalogue style. It took a moment to realise that Ben was frowning at me.

"Well, what do you think?" I'd asked him.

"It's ok," he said slowly, and the girls stopped their chorus of oos and Ahhs to listen to his analysis. His face broke into a sly smile, "I'm not sure the general public is ready for those calf muscles. Unless you are planning to join the Russian Olympic wrestling team." he said with a snigger. My heart sank. The girls started to giggle, following their father's lead so I tried to put a brave face on it.

"It looks fine, honestly." he said, "They just make you look a bit, ummmm...chunky." The girls laughed proper belly laughs. I was stood at the front of the living room in front of my family, feeling extremely foolish, but because I don't want to make my daughters feel bad for mocking me, I forced a laugh too. It was all I could do to stop myself crying.

"Bit chunkilicious, eh?" I said and they all burst into uproarious laughter. "Ok, maybe not this one then." I walked back up to the bedroom, taking off the clothes and the boots and carefully placing them back in the bags, pulling out the receipts and tucking them in my jean pockets. I got changed back into my old clothes, having lost all appetite for trying on any of the other purchases from the day. I piled up the carrier bags by the front door ready to be loaded back into the car and then headed into the kitchen to boil the kettle. Ben, who had started on the dinner, looked past me out into the hallway.

"What are you doing with those?" he asked.

"Taking them back." I said avoiding looking at him. My throat felt tight like the tears were coming but I refused to cry in front of him.

"Why?" he asked, and I could tell he was genuinely surprised. Anger gave me the strength I needed to look him in the eye.

"Because you laughed at me." I said.

"Oh, don't be so juvenile. Take them back upstairs."

"No. You wouldn't want to wear clothes that people had laughed at you in, would you?"

"Probably." he said with an indifferent shrug.

"Don't talk bollocks Ben, of course you wouldn't." I said finishing making my cup of tea, I tucked my new paperback under my arm and headed into the lounge. I curled up on the sofa with my tea and my book, which I could not concentrate on because I was too busy trying to figure out if I really was overreacting or if my husband was actually a bit of a dick.

14

I was standing on the corner of Normandy Street watching the rush hour traffic amble up to the roundabout in the early evening gloom, my heavy winter coat doing little to keep out the arctic wind and my cheeks bright red with frostbite. The tall white building opposite was lit up with spotlights, but the paint was crumbling, and the Cinema sign crooked. I thought, I must remember to tell Alex he needs to get the sign seen to before it falls on someone's head. Alex had owned The Palace Cinema since he inherited it from his Uncle in the early nineties. He'd invested his life savings into the venture, desperate to save the art deco building and the small, independent cinema that was housed within.

For a while it had looked like he might pull it off and the locals flocked to the little screens. For the first time since the seventies it was making a profit and Alex had ploughed every last penny into underpinning the drooping foundations, plastering the old brick facade and updating all of the projectors. Time moves fast in the cinema industry though and all of the new technology was out of date in the blink of an eye, just as sales started to dip dramatically. It had been a downward spiral and no amount of special offers or cinema clubs could bring back the loyal customer base he needed just to keep on top of the bills.

Alex and I had been friends for two years. Close friends, but just friends all the same. Monday evenings had been about just him and me on the back row, munching on popcorn and laughing like lunatics. Often there would be no-one else in the place, and so he would lock the front doors and we would put our feet up on the seats in front like a couple of unruly kids, giving our own running commentary on the films in loud voices. He was the teenage boyfriend I had never had, although I hasten to add there had been no funny business. Absolutely no kissing or touching; just a couple of friends having a laugh at the cinema, like you do. That's not to say I hadn't wanted to though. Sometimes in the gloom at the back of the room, I had turned to watch his face as the light from the screen flickered across his features. I could just look at him and feel this curious warmth spread across my chest. He was an unmistakably beautiful man, but perpetually single and I could never quite figure out why. Perhaps the cinema was too much of an albatross around his neck and he felt duty bound to go down with this particular sinking ship. I wished I could do something to help him, besides being the most consistently dedicated customer for the past two years.

It felt strange, stood on the cold street corner, that I hadn't seen him for the best part of a month. I took a deep breath, stopping long enough to watch my breath dissipate into the cold night and stepped forward to cross the road. Inside was a short flight of steps to a little kiosk. Quite often, Alex would rope in his ancient mother to man the front desk, particularly on the busier nights and I wondered sadly if the Monday's since Ben had died had been complete no-shows. I got my answer when I got to the kiosk. Alex was slouched forward, staring miserably at his mobile and didn't look up as I approached.

"Could I have one ticket for the eight pm please." I said and he looked up with a jolt, almost falling off his stool. His green eyes blinked at me as if he couldn't quite believe that I was there and I smiled shyly. My heart was thundering. He was wearing a thick grey jumper and I couldn't help but think how wonderful it would feel to be cuddled up in his arms, the soft wool against my cheek. He regained his composure slowly and a cheeky smile crept across his face.

"Would that be a senior ticket Madam?" he asked. It was our running joke. He teased me relentlessly because I whinged relentlessly about how old I felt. He would always tell me it was ridiculous that I should feel like that, but he still took any opportunity to poke fun at me.

"Cheeky." I said, the smile on my face felt unfamiliar. It had been a while. I slid a five-pound note across the counter like I always did, and he slid it straight back to me as he always did. He grabbed a big bag of popcorn for us to share, keys jangling as he walked to lock the front door. Skipping back up the steps towards me, he offered for me to take his arm. I looped my arm around his and we squeezed each other tight.

The theatre was deathly cold, and Alex apologised.

"I wasn't expecting anyone to be in tonight. The heating hasn't been on for a month." He said disappearing out into the corridor and returning with a tiny fan heater. It was noisy and barely cut through the glacial feel in the cinema, but I didn't care. I had come prepared and was wearing all my thermals and my thickest winter coat. "I'll be two minutes. We're showing Black Gun tonight, is that ok?" he asked.

"I honestly don't care." I said eliciting his most gloriously boyish of smiles. I heard his footsteps thump up the stairs behind me to the projectionist's booth. I had asked him to take me up there many times in the past, but he refused each time, swearing it would ruin the magic, but I suspected the truth was it might be dangerous for us to be alone in the tiny room together. Within moments, the screen flickered to life and I heard him thumping his way back to me. He sat beside me and we turn to each other and smiled. This feels right, I thought, this is my happy place, here with him. The film started and we looked to the screen.

"I've missed you." He whispered into my ear and the tears pricked my eyes. He found my hand in the darkness, his was warm and soft.

"Me too." I said. We sat and watched the film in contented silence, just enjoying each other's existence beside one another, not daring to let go of each other's hands. Not even to shovel popcorn into our mouths, the pot stayed wedged between my leg and the edge of my seat.

Before long we were making our usual sarcastic commentary and scathing criticism of the film, the plot and the actors. We rather fancied ourselves as serious film critics, although we were agreed that it was unlikely that anyone would really be interested in our opinions, so we kept them between us. The main character, an older female actress appeared on the screen and I gasped.

"She's so beautiful...she must be about sixty now...but she looks about twenty-three!" I said. Alex guffawed.

"Yeah...twenty-three...minutes from death. Jesus, look at the state of her." I laughed, "I don't understand how you can be so down on yourself and yet find that attractive!" he pointed to the screen, but he was looking at me. I looked back at him and it was one of those dangerous moments. We've had so many before. I was sure we could both feel the desire to lean forward and just kiss. This was the first time since my husband died and anxiety was roaring through my bloodstream. It was just too soon. I swallowed hard and turned back to the screen, hearing him sighing softly beside me.

I'm sorry, I thought, wishing he could hear my thoughts. I tilted my head and rested it on his shoulder. He slipped down a little into his seat to make it more comfortable for me and rested his head on mine. We both sighed heavily and then laughed at each other. Neither of us were really watching the film, it was just a front to be able to spend time together. I liked to imagine that his mind was a whirl of "What now?" just like mine. I felt a momentary sense of hope, that something good might come out of this terrible situation and it was instantly replaced by crushing guilt and self-loathing.

"I've seen Ben." I said and Alex jerked up in his seat, turning to look at me.

"What?" he said.

"I've seen him. Or rather I've seen his ghost. And I've spoken with him. Quite a lot in fact, in the last week or so." I couldn't meet his eyes, so I picked at the bobbled fabric on the arm of the theatre seat. Alex reached forward and tilted my face up with his finger under my chin. This was the conversation that I had been dreading having.

"Have you gone mental?" Alex asked. He always smouldered when he looked serious. It was devastatingly handsome, but I was feeling too hopeless to enjoy it. All I could do was shake my head. Suddenly he sat up straighter in his seat and looked around "Is he here now?" I noticed he took barely a second to doubt my judgement or think me insane. This man had an unwavering trust in me. I looked around the dark theatre, but more than anything I trusted in my senses.

"He's not here now. Would it make a difference if he was?" I asked, searching Alex's face for a reaction.

"Guess not." He said relaxing a little. "What's he going to do about it?" We settled back into our little embrace, even though the film had finished, and the screen was black. The room was dark and cold and smelt ever so slightly of damp, but we were warm in each other's company. Just as I was thinking I could happily stay there all night, happily enduring the inevitable frostbite, my phone beeped. The phone lit up my face in the dark and I was cringingly aware it would highlight every crack and wrinkle, so I tried to turn away from Alex. It was only a text message from Becky wondering when I would be home, apparently Nanna was threatening to pluck her eyebrows and she was prepared to use physical violence to stop her if necessary.

"I have to go." I said to Alex and his face dropped. Somehow, it didn't seem to matter how much time we snatched together, it was never enough.

"Ok." He said giving my hand a final squeeze

before letting it go. The cold swept in and I felt frozen to the bone. He walked me back to the entrance in silence. He turned the key in the lock and pushed open the door to let me out. I stepped out onto the pavement and turned to face him. He looked unbearably sad and I just wanted to take him in my arms. I sneaked a look up and down the road and feeling uncharacteristically brave slipped my arms around his waist, pulling him into my embrace. He wrapped his arms around me. I felt the tenderest kiss on top of my forehead. I couldn't bear to leave him, so I tore myself out of the hug and marched head down away from him without looking back. The walk home was cold and dark. I stopped by the church where the candle lights blazed through the stained-glass windows and a choir practising Christmas hymns filled the night with a festive air that did nothing to cheer me up. I strode on past the church and the graveyard as cars flew past drenching me in bright headlights before plunging me into darkness again. As I turned into Greenfields Avenue Ben appeared before me in much the same state as the first time I had seen him after he had died.

"Trace, you've got to get home now!" he shouted.

"What's wrong? Is it the girls?" I felt panic rising.

"The gas is on, your Dad has fallen asleep, you've got to get home now!" he shouted, and I broke into a run. I was out of breath within a few seconds, but the adrenaline kicked in and I pumped my chubby legs as fast as I could. Ben was beside me the whole way.

"It's her. The little girl." He said.

"What? Why? We said we'd do it!" I panted.

"Did you email the woman though? Did you

actually set something up?"

"No!" I croaked. Why was she doing this to us! Suddenly the idea of collaborating with this malicious spirit seemed like a terrible idea, but then what choice did we have?

I fumbled my keys out of my pocket and groaned as I dropped them on the floor. Ben's spirit was behind me, pleading with me to hurry. Finally, I flew into the house, leaving the front door open as I rushed into the lounge. I could smell the thick gas that had filled the room. Dad was snoring on the sofa, his hands rested on his tummy.

"Dad!" I screeched and he startled and woke. I pulled off the front plate of the fireplace and twisted the gas off.

"What the hell, love?" Dad stood up, "Christ, is that gas I can smell?" He turned pale. The girls and my Mum come running down the stairs just as I was opening all the windows and trying to waft all of the gas out of the room. "I didn't touch the fire, I swear. Girls, did you touch the fire?" They both shook their heads.

"It's ok, it's ok." I said.

"But, what the hell is going on?" Dad was shouting but not in anger, in fear. We could all sense that something was not quite right and in my panic I couldn't think how I would explain this to them. A black shape caught my eye. She was standing in the shadows and I could just about make out her form.

"It's ok." I repeated, to her this time though, "I will sort it now". She faded into the shadows around her.

15

The next morning, I opened the door to find two peculiar men on my doorstep. The first I initially mistook for a Jehovah's witness of some variety. He was short and slight, dressed in plain blue chinos and a cream shirt under his heavy waxed jacket. His face was dominated by brown rimmed circular glasses with thick lenses. On the top of his head was a wide, round bald patch, the brown hair beyond it having been allowed to grow long and thick giving it the appearance of a voluminous halo around the shiny hair-free patch. The man's companion towered, standing at a little distance behind him. His thick dark hair was gelled up into a gentle quiff and a short black beard rested regally on his chin. Whilst he was undeniably of the Caucasian persuasion, he was dressed in a pink kimono emblazoned with elaborate twisting dragons. Strapped to his back was a very long and very sharp looking samurai sword. I looked from one to the other, their faces were impassive and calm.

"Errr…hello?" My confused brain considered momentarily that the local churches were really making an effort to recruit these days.

"Hello Tracey." Said the first man, his voice had

a nasal quality and he was quietly spoken. "May we come in for a chat?"

"Sorry who are you? And how do you know my name?" A sense of foreboding would have been perfectly natural at this time, however, there was such a calmness about the pair my instincts were telling me to let them in and I was struggling with this.

"My name is Kevin," the first man said, "and this is my spirit guide Timothy." Timothy nodded sagely. His form had been so perfectly solid that it hadn't occurred to me for a second that he might not be of this plain of living.

"Right." I said, "I guess you had better come in then." I stepped aside and Kevin took his time to wipe his feet meticulously on the door mat before moving into the hallway. Timothy moved in after him, his sword swiping through the walls as he walked. His intimidating bulk stood at least two foot taller than me and it hurt my neck to look up at him. I lead them into the lounge. I sat on one edge of the corner sofa, while they sat beside one another on the other end. Kevin looked miniscule beside his spirit guide. We stared at each other in an awkward silence for several moments, during which Timothy let out a slightly dainty cough and Kevin appeared to be scanning me for information. I wasn't quite sure what to say.

"You are probably wondering why we are here?" Kevin said. I raised an eyebrow, hoping I was conveying my thoughts; no shit. "As you have probably guessed I am a psychic medium."

"And I am his spirit guide." Announced Timothy in a booming and reverent voice.

"Yes, she knows that, I already told her." Kevin added with a note of irritation to his voice.

"Oh sorry."

"It's fine, just…" Kevin made a motion with his hands as if pushing Timothy back, imploring him to back off. "As I was saying, I am a psychic medium and Timothy is my spirit guide. We understand that you have recently acquired some psychic ability. In a manner of speaking?"

"I can see dead people." I blurted out.

"Okay don't do that." Kevin jumped in, "That's not cool. That's not how we do things. There's a certain decorum to our profession. One that can take many, many years of training and mentoring. For example, I was trained from the age of seven by my Great Aunt. She herself had been taught by her own mother. It is a noble and ancient calling, that only the purest are born into. It is very unusual for someone to acquire 'the gift' at such an advanced age. No offence." Timothy continued nodding sagely whilst gently stroking his tiny, chin-beard. It occurred to me that he was surprisingly camp for such a burly man, spirit, ghost-thing.

"Sorry, how did you know I had acquired the gift and why are you here exactly?" I said trying not to let my irritation become too obvious.

"Well, you've been causing a bit of a stir in the afterlife, I'm afraid. Your reading with Cheryl didn't go so well we heard." Timothy harrumphed as if to suggest that might have been an understatement, which it was, but that didn't stop me being pissed off. It seemed to me that there might be some kind of psychic elite and they were here to tell me that I wasn't pure enough to be a member of the club.

"It might not have gone well, but I don't think that was anything to with me not being good enough. Nobody could have predicted that her mother would be so evil. That was hardly my fault!" Kevin and Timothy exchanged a look.

"Listen, I don't mean to sound patronising," Kevin said in the most patronising tone I had heard in my life, "but this isn't the kind of thing that you can just jump into. Dealing with people spirit side is...well...diplomatically challenging."

"I had noticed." I added icily.

"I understand that your husband passed over recently. Quite suddenly." He said in a change of tack. I nodded. It was still a bit raw. "I'm sorry for your loss, it must have been quite a shock." I looked down at my hands in my lap.

"It was horrific." I said in a small voice.

"The fact that he was able to come down to the earthly plane so quickly after passing is a testament to the devotion he felt towards you and your children. It's no mean feat, particularly after such a sudden passing. But there was clearly a reason he needed to be close to you."

"It felt like my prayers had been answered. I wasn't ready to lose him. Seeing him again was as if I hadn't really lost him at all." I said. Kevin's expression was hard to read but he exchanged a look with Timothy that made me think there might some bad news to come. It occurred to me that, besides the telling off I was almost certainly about to receive, these chaps could actually help me a little, so it might be wise to get them on side. "Oh, how rude of me! I haven't offered you a cup of tea, would you like a drink?" I asked Kevin.

"A cup of tea would be lovely." Said Kevin and then he lowered his voice to a whisper, "And an empty cup for Timothy please if it's no trouble?" While he said this, Timothy looked away coquettishly. I returned a few minutes later with two steaming cups and one empty one, which Timothy accepted with a smile and a nod of the head. He crossed his bulky legs and lifted the cup to his lips, his pinky raised.

"He doesn't like to feel left out." Kevin added quietly. I smiled and nodded, trying not to let it show how weird I found it.

"Okay, so before you give me a ticking off, I just want to say that I have vowed never to do a personal reading again." I said.

"We know." Said Kevin. "That's not why we are here. Although, I have to emphasise how reckless it was for you to jump straight in like that. These kinds of things have to be handled with such delicacy, you could have done some very real damage. Luckily, I don't think you have in this instance." I was inwardly wincing throughout. He wasn't telling me anything I didn't already know, but it still felt deeply unpleasant.

"I know. I'm sorry." I was suitably chastened and hoped that would be the end of it. "I absolutely guarantee that it will never happen again." Timothy and Kevin seemed to accept this with relative equanimity as if they had already bored of the topic of conversation. "So can I ask, why are you here?" I was surprised when Kevin looked suddenly abashed and suddenly less certain of himself.

"Well, it's a little bit awkward actually." He paused and I had to admit my interest was piqued. "I'm just going to come out with it. We're having a bit of a rebrand of our marketing and we've been struggling a little bit. I couldn't help but notice your Facebook book page. It's really rather good, despite the fact you have spelt psychic wrong...many times...and in many different ways. Basically, I was just wondering if we could get some help?" I could only sit and stare and the strange little medium and his ginormous friend while what he said sank in. I figured why the hell not.

"Yeah sure. I can do that!" I said, thinking it would be a piece of piss.

Two hours of discussing colour schemes, logos and wording later, I was ready to concede that it was not, in fact, going to be a piece of piss. Although I had managed to eject the unusual pair from my house before the girls got home from school. Before he left, Kevin turned to me and eyeballed me curiously. I had been avoiding the topic of the job at the Crown all afternoon, hoping he wouldn't try to talk me out of that too. I needed the money too desperately to walk away.

"The job at the Crown is right for you." He finally said. Apparently, it was futile to try and hide anything from a psychic.

"What if I cock it up? Like Cheryl's reading." I whimpered, my confidence in tatters.

"You won't. This is something you need to do. Have faith in yourself and trust your instincts." His smile was warm.

16

My first appointment with Erin was arranged for the following afternoon. I stressed the urgency and could imagine that if this malign spirit was causing similar issues at The Crown, then there could well be a family with a young child in serious danger. Thankfully, Erin was as desperate to see me as I was her and I felt a little ashamed to have dithered unnecessarily. Before my appointment, however, I was in need of sustenance and fortifying company, so I called up Immy and we arranged to meet for a coffee. The Bean was our normal haunt, right at the top of the high street, away from the riffraff (Immy's words not mine) with some ridiculously comfy sofas at the back that we normally commandeered if we could. Their mocha was killer, and their chocolate fudge cake came with a type 2 diabetes disclaimer.

I spent the entire morning dithering, generally trying to put the brakes on my day so I didn't have to face up to what was coming that afternoon, but also, I couldn't decide what, if anything, I would tell Immy about what was going on. She already knew a lot about Alex and suspected more had happened, even though it hadn't. She was of the opinion, before his sudden departure to the spiritual realm, that I should leave Ben and run away with Alex. I suggested that she had been reading too many trashy romance novels. Life is never that simple; there is no happy ending. I also stressed my innocence, proclaiming we'd never so much as kissed and it was the truth, but god how I'd wanted too. I wasn't exactly clear on what the protocol was when you meet a man you felt an amazing connection with, but you were already unhappily married to someone else? And then what if your husband suddenly died, but then he showed up in ghost form? There's no manual for situations like that. I had already checked on Amazon.

When I arrived at The Bean, my sister was sat with her legs tucked under her on one of the leather sofas, chatting happily to a young man. He was sat on the arm of the chair gazing happily into her voluminous cleavage and she was looking up at him with a playful grin on her face, pretending to be ten years younger than she was. I slumped down onto the seat opposite her, feeling impossibly frumpy and was largely ignored for some time. It was only once he had her phone number typed into his mobile, that he left us and she turned her attention to me.

"Coffee?" I asked wearily and she drained the remains of her cup and handed it to me. I pulled myself back out of the chair with great effort and a bit of a groan. At the counter, I counted my blessings that this was not one of the places where I had begged for a job, placing an order for two large mochas with Kate the red-faced, slightly harassed barista. She took my money, my last dogeared ten-pound note, and told me she would bring them over when they were ready.

I flung myself back into the sofa and moaned loudly to ensure that Immy was fully aware of my emotional suffering and was prepared to bring the support and attention that I needed. I looked up to see that she had raised an eyebrow in askance but that appeared to be as far as she was willing to go.

"I'm suffering Immy. Really suffering." I said pathetically.

"Not still going on about your dead husband, are you? God, it's been weeks already." She rolled her eyes. I stopped and thought for a second. I should probably, by rights, have still been miserable about my poor dead husband, it had only been a few weeks. Somehow, though, this seemed to be the least of my worries.

"No, actually, Although I am still sad about that obviously."

"Of course!" she said sarcastically.

"Of course." I said firmly, "I'm in despair for many, many reasons. But mainly because I saw Alex last night." I had captured her interest and she pulled her feet out from under her to sit forward in her chair.

"So, you're finally getting it on with dishy Alex. Well done you, little sister. It's about time!"

"No, we are not getting it on. It's far too soon, I can't be jumping into bed with another man!"

"Why not? Who would know about it? And more to the point, who would actually care?"

"Umm...Ben and Ben I would say."

"Yeah but how would he know? He is dead!" she said, rather insensitively I thought, but then that was Immy all over. Always ready to call a spade a spade.

"He would know, because he's still here." She stopped halfway through sipping her coffee and just stared at me. She appeared to be quietly assessing my mental state. "I've seen him." Her frown deepened.

"You think you've seen him?" She suggested.

"Nope, I have definitely, actually seen him and spoken with him."

"As in you've seen him alive and walking about and he's not actually dead?" she asked.

"No, as in very much dead, materialising as a ghost and talking to me from the other side."

"Oh." She said. "Are you sure you're not just going a bit mad?" I never tired of being asked that question.

"Not really." I glugged some coffee enthusiastically as if it might be wine and considered for a moment. It would have been an actual relief to know I had gone mad and this was all a construction of my confused, depressed mind. The evidence was stacked against this hypothesis, however. For a start I felt completely sane, not that any self-respecting mad woman would have said otherwise. Also, Ben had accurately predicted where I would find the logbook and how to open the glovebox. I couldn't have figured that out by myself. Also, if the spirits that pitched up to Cheryl's reading were a figment of my imagination then I would never have been able to give her the scant information that I had for her reading. It occurred to me then that the girl with no eyes must also be real and I felt a shiver snake up my spine. Unfortunately, it seemed that I was not going mad. "Okay, I'm pretty sure I'm not going mad." I said. Immy raised her eyebrows to show she was not convinced.

"So, what did he have to say for himself?" She obviously blamed him for all of my woes, which seemed a bit harsh. It wasn't as if he died out of choice.

"A few things actually. He's been trying to help me set up my new business." I said hoping she wouldn't probe further, but she just sat and stared me down. "We're professional paranormal investigators." Immy burst out laughing. She was so loud practically everyone in the cafe turned to look at us.

"What the actual..."

"Immy no." I jumped in. A mother sat with her young toddler was staring daggers at us.

"Seriously, Tracey, of all the things you could have done! You really are nuts."

"I'm going to see our first paying customer this afternoon." I mumbled. "Please stop laughing. I was desperate and there's this ghost girl and she's desperate for us to help this family, so I have to do it really."

"Completely nuts." She was looking quite concerned now, "You need to see a doctor or something Trace."

"I'm not mad."

"You've just lost your husband and you're presented with the perfect opportunity to be with the man of your dreams, your soul mate if you will, but instead you decide to start hanging around haunted houses with your dead husband? That sounds pretty nuts to me." She sipped her coffee, never taking her eyes off me, her look disapproving, like I had some choice in the way things had worked out.

"I can't control what Ben does. He just turns up whenever he wants, or whatever."

"And you still saw Alex last night though?"

"I know, I just...I couldn't go any longer without seeing him." I said.

"And how did Ben feel about this? Does he know?" She sat forward again.

"Ben didn't show up, but then all I did was go to

the cinema and Alex just happened to be there, sat beside me, holding my hand." I blushed deeper.

"Right, here's what you need to do." Good old Immy always kept her head in a crisis, "You need to tell Ben about Alex and you need to get it together with Alex. Then, you need to get yourself a proper bloody job." I just stared at her for a minute or two taking on board what she had said. I had expected something a bit less stark to be honest.

"You make it sound so easy." I said, "It's never that easy."

"It can be if you want it to be." She shrugged and sat back in the seat. "Life's too short to be miserable. It could all be over tomorrow. You of all people should know this." Her look was stern, but still I thought, it's never that easy. I looked at my watch.

"I've got to go." I said standing to put on my coat, "Wish me luck?"

"I will not!" she scoffed, but she stood and hugged me anyway, "Stay safe little Sis. And call me later to let me know how you get on, you big nutcase."

I arrived at The Crown Inn to find Ben was already there, stood on the opposite side of the road watching the building intently. As far as pubs went it was a pretty standard brick-built pub, although their website stated it was over four hundred years old, it had looked more Georgian in style to me; tall and grand, with wide sash windows and brightly painted rendering. It stood on the corner at the top of the high street, the road to St Lawrence's church ran along it's right side and the ancient church itself peeking out from behind the crooked walls of the pub. At that point I had never actually ventured into The Crown, although in fairness I had rarely ventured out socially at all in the past two decades. Even still, it felt strange to be so unfamiliar even though it was practically on my doorstep.

"Did you get the chance to check it out." I asked and Ben nodded slowly.

"Couldn't sense anything in there, which is a bit odd." I looked at him. "Well, it's a pretty old building. You would expect there to be plenty of spirits in there wouldn't you" He was right, and this revelation unsettled me. I turned back to the building and spotted a face at the top right-hand window. The face of a little girl. Where her eyes should have been there was nothing but dark gaping holes.

17

Erin greeted me at the back door. She was friendly but nervous and seemed to be on constant alert, flipping her head round at the slightest noise or movement behind her. She was the kind of woman that I would have been jealous of having around my husband ordinarily, with her slim waist, long, brown hair and naturally beautiful face; I don't normally trust women who put that much effort into growing their hair so long but something about her was disarming enough to put me at ease. My old college friend, Lisa, had ruined long hair for me. Without fail, on every girly night out she had been flocked by men, drawn in by her bum length blonde hair and startling blue eyes, while I would be ignored despite the unmistakable fact that I outboobed her on every level. At one point, even Ben had tried his luck with lovely Lisa, while I sat in the corner nursing a lurid blue alcopop and my own simmering resentment. Needless to say, he didn't get far. Lisa went on to marry an insurance salesman from Woking and was living the suburban dream with three bouncing children and a horrifying mortgage.

Erin ushered me through into a dark corridor and then into the main part of the restaurant. Dark wood tables arranged neatly around the room which stylistically belonged in the mid to late nineties, were fully laid out for guests. We walked through this room into a small corridor, passing a staircase down to a basement, the door to our left was the main entrance onto the high street which was shut. Another low door led into a large bar room. Thick black beams crossed the ceiling and formed a partial wall jutting out into the centre of the room, where I suspected a wall had been dismantled, the wooden struts left in place to create a small nook in the far end of the room. Standard issue, sticky topped pub tables dotted across a strategically dark, heavily patterned blue carpet; ideal for concealing decades of spillage and suchlike. The bar ran along the right-hand side of the room and into the far corner. On the far wall a small fireplace was stacked with logs. Behind the bar two men were deep in discussion. The older man was sipping from a pint of beer, which he picked up and carried over to Erin and I, whilst the younger man flicked lazily through a catalogue, seemingly making an effort to ignore us. His bare arms were covered in thick black tattoos and his face was full of studs and rings.

"Hi, you must be Tracey." the man said holding out his hand. He reeked of beer. I told myself he'd probably just been fixing a leaky barrel, but the red rimmed eyes and shaking hands were a dead giveaway. I'd seen this before and, unfortunately, I was well qualified in spotting an alcoholic when I saw one. Ben's father had only been a part of our lives for a short time, but his influence still lingered nearly twenty years after his death.

"This is my husband Matt," said Erin, standing a little closer to him as if seeking his protection. Or perhaps seeking to protect him. I reached out to shake his hand and smiled at them both. They made a handsome couple, despite Matt's apparent issues, and I placed them in their early or mid-thirties.

"Lovely to meet you." I said trying not to show how unnerved the intense atmosphere of the place was making me feel. "Perhaps you could start by telling me a bit about what's been going on?" We sat at a table near the fireplace. I could feel a bitter draft seeping through the gaps in the window behind me and I shivered. The young man from the bar appeared suddenly beside us, his eyes were thick dark brown, almost black.

"Let me get that fire going for you." He said. His friendliness took me off guard. His posture, eyes and aura were giving off an altogether more hostile energy.

"Thanks Rob." Said Erin. I suspected he was only tending the fire so that he could eavesdrop on the conversation, nosy bastard. Ben was still upstairs trying to track down the girl we saw at the window, which I had sent him to do under duress.

"Well, I don't really know where to start." Matt said laying his hands open, face down on the table and then gripping them together again. "We've been here...what...three months now? The brewery had to evict the last leaseholders because they were behind on the rent. We took on the place probably a couple of months after they left."

"We were both teachers." She added, "The hours were ridiculous, we were stressed and unhappy. So when my Gran passed away and we found out she had left me her house in her will, we finally had the means to do something that would give us a bit of work-life balance while Natalie is growing up. I don't think we realised just how unhappy we had been until we came here and for a while, we were so excited and happy that we had had the guts to do this." I was nodding and smiling in an attempt to put them at ease, but I didn't want to interrupt them. Everything they were telling me could potentially be relevant. "It took us a few months to sell Gran's house and by then we had found this place and it just seemed perfect. We scheduled two months for the renovations and during that whole time there were no issues whatsoever. We had workmen and decorators in constantly and no-one had any problems, nothing strange happened at all."

"It's only when we got close to opening, things got a bit odd." said Matt, "it's like the whole atmosphere in the place changed overnight." Erin nodded vigorously.

"It was so strange. I can't even explain it. There was just this feeling of...there being something there. And it was colder, it just felt colder in every room, although that could have just been the weather turning. Oh, I don't know. It feels so ridiculous saying this to you now." She said, her eyes searching my face as if trying to pick up on whether I believed her or not, and I sensed she was hoping that I would tell her she was being ridiculous and that everything was absolutely fine. No ghosts here! Unfortunately, I couldn't. I could, however, feel that there was something wrong in this place, but until Ben got back, I couldn't tell her this categorically. The basic human condition is highly impressionable, and there is every likelihood that being told I was going to a haunted place with a strange atmosphere that I would feel convinced there was something creepy going on. I needed some insider knowledge before I jumped to conclusions. So, I just nodded and smiled and hoped Erin and Matt didn't think I was a simpleton.

"No, I felt it too." Said Matt wrapping an arm around his wife, "And so did Nats. Natalie is our daughter by the way. She's only five and frankly I'm amazed that she can bear to be in the place. I begged her to go and stay with my mother in law until this has all been sorted but she refuses to leave. I don't know if she's seen anything, but then I don't want to ask her because I don't want to frighten her."

"So, what kinds of occurrences have you experienced? And what have you seen?" I asked.

"Until very recently, it has been the staff that have been affected more than us." Said Matt. "We've lost every single member of staff, except Robin." Having finished building up the fire, Robin stood beside the table.

"I haven't actually seen anything." He said with a slightly unsettling smile and a shrug, before walking back to the bar.

"We've had waitresses saying that they felt someone take their hand, but there was no-one there." said Erin. "We've had others tell us they heard a small child whispering when they were all alone in the cellar. One of the chefs said he saw a figure passing by the kitchen door but when he looked there was no-one there. Most of them said they had felt like there was something watching them, they said it was just a feeling but at the end of the day they had felt so frightened by the feeling, they wouldn't come back."

"One of the girls, a sous-chef called Isla, said that she had seen a little girl. To be honest we were relieved when she left, she was absolutely useless and my god, what an attitude problem! But she told us she'd seen a figure in the corner of her eye and had thought it was Nats at first, but then when she turned to talk to her...well Isla said," Erin lowered her voice to a whisper, "she had no eyes." I felt struck cold, as if I'd had a bucket of ice poured over my head. I needed Ben's help to find out who this girl was and why she was doing this and fast. Erin and Matt registered my reaction and shared a look, their faces grim.

"I have seen the girl with no eyes." I said, trying to project an air of mystery that would convince them to put their faith in me and my non-existent abilities. "I can help, but I'm going to need some time." I said. They nodded enthusiastically, their relief palpable.

"Honestly, anything you can do, we would be so grateful. We're at our wits end." Said Erin and I could see she was close to tears. Matt looked less convinced but seemed to be giving me the benefit of the doubt.

"Perhaps you could start by showing me around?" I asked. So that I can find my fecking useless husband, I added to myself.

"Sure," Erin said, standing. We left Matt who slunk straight back to the bar with the half empty pint glass. Erin and I passed through the way we had come, stopping in the little restaurant area. Erin explained how they had been hoping to build up the food side of the business separately and try to divert the "riff-raff" into the sports bar in the basement, leaving the main bar for a better class of clientele. I tried not to grimace, revealing my doubts as to her plans; this was not the time to reveal my inner snob. The room felt peculiarly still, as rooms that are custom built to be humming with people are wont to do when devoid of life. We stood in silence for a moment while I tried to urge my senses to pick out anything out of the ordinary, but as Ben already told me, the place was quiet as a grave. I suggested that Erin took me down to the cellar, where I had read online in my scant research, that there was a resident ghost called Patrick.

"We're calling this the Sports Bar," Erin explained as we made our way down the cramped staircase and into the cellar. She flipped on the light and I saw that part of what I presumed had been the beer cellar, had been converted into another drinking area, with the bar in the centre and high tables and stools dotted about between a pool table and darts board. "We thought it might be good for when there are big football games on, and better for the other customers to keep the rowdiness contained. The beer cellar is through there." She pointed to a door behind us but didn't open it. The atmosphere in the cellar was claustrophobic and I felt no urge to explore any further. My head was starting to throb, although whether that was something paranormal or just the stress of keeping up my charade I didn't know.

I said nothing and Erin led me back up the stairs and then through the restaurant to the back of the inn, where the stairs led up to the first floor. As I followed her upwards, I couldn't help but admire how Erin's skin-tight jeans seemed to cling effortlessly to her slim body. I thought to myself, I would give anything to have a figure like that...well anything except not stuffing my face with donuts and biscuits. By the time we reached the next floor I was trying to hide the fact I was flustered and panting slightly. Erin seemed oblivious.

The entire floor was a rabbit's warren of hotel rooms. We swept up and down the corridor, craning around doors at the rooms fully made up ready for guests. All except one; the door to twenty-three was locked and we passed the shut door without comment.

Another set of stairs took us up to the staff quarters in the attic, where Erin, Matt and Natalie were living. Instantly the atmosphere changed. Erin was prattling through the rooms, telling me what each was used for as if it weren't fairly obvious, but I was becoming restless and stressed. I was completely out of my depth here. I needed Ben's help if I was going to be able to help this family. We were in the corridor when we heard the scream.

"Natalie." Gasped Erin and she ran to the end of the small flat. I was seconds behind her when we hurtled through the door to a little girl's bedroom. It had a new paint smell; the walls were a delicate pink, the furniture crisp white and toys were neatly arranged everywhere I looked. On the bed a little girl was hugging her knees tight.

"The man! The man!" she pointed to the far corner of the room where I could see Ben stood awkwardly, his hands raised defensively and a grimace on his face.

"I was just trying to talk to her." He said to me. Natalie screamed again. Her mother was sat beside her on her bed hugging her tight and looking wide-eyed around the room in a panic.

"It's okay." I said keeping my voice low and even, "It's just my spirit guide Ben. He doesn't want to harm you." Whilst Erin looked visibly relieved, Natalie had buried her faces into her mother's shoulder. I looked to Ben and nodded my head to the left. He got the message and disappeared. "I'm just going to give you a moment." I said to Erin and hurried out into the corridor where Ben was waiting for me.

"That didn't go well!" he looked shocked.

"What the hell were you doing!?" I asked in a

frantic whisper.

"The girl with no eyes took me to her. She said I needed to talk to her, so I tried to."

"Did she say anything?" I asked.

"No, she just freaked out." he looked genuinely shaken.

"Great, so what now?" I said rubbing my temples. I was exasperated and exhausted already.

"You need to try and talk to her and see what she says." He said. "Whatever is going on here, is something to do with her." Fat lot of help he was turning out to be, I thought. I headed back into the bedroom, where Natalie seemed calmer and was sat on her mother's lap. Erin was shushing her and looked up to me eagerly as I came back into the room. I sat on the bedroom floor on the soft unicorn rug next to the bed.

"I'm sorry the man scared you Natalie," I said, "He really was just trying to help. He didn't mean to upset you." Natalie looked back at me with devastatingly beautiful, big blue eyes. The weight of the responsibility on me became that little bit more crushing and I winced inwardly.

"He scared me." She said dragging her sleeve across her eyes.

"I'm sorry sweetie. He's a daft old thing." She laughed at that and we all relaxed a little. "Do you mind if I talk to you?" she nodded, and I looked to Erin who nodded too.

"Natalie hasn't seen anything that we know of." Said Erin quietly and I saw Natalie shoot her mother a look that suggested otherwise. I had to tread carefully to get her to open up to me, but also to make sure I didn't put the fear of god into the poor little thing.

"Okay," I said thinking hard how to approach

this. "How are you liking your new home Natalie?" I asked with what I hoped passed for a disarming smile.

"Well, I like being in the attic. I can see the whole street from my bedroom. Yesterday some men came to put up the Christmas lights. One of them almost fell off the thing that lifted him up." She giggled. "Our new house is loads bigger than our old house. I like it here because I can play hide and seek. Sometimes I play with my friend." I shared a look with Erin.

"That's nice, is she a new friend?" I asked. Natalie nodded.

"Her name is Fanny." I could hear Ben sniggering from the hallway and Erin looked puzzled.

"Wow, that's a very...unusual name." She said.

"She's here sometimes and we play games and I let her play with my toys." Said Natalie and Erin startled.

"She's been up to your room?" she asked watching her daughter's face as it crumpled with concern.

"Sometimes." Natalie's eyes welled up, "Have I done something wrong Mummy?"

"No darling, it's fine." Erin hugged her daughter a little harder, "Just we don't want customers coming upstairs into our bit of the inn do we." I had thought we had all come to the conclusion that this little girl was no customer, but Natalie wasn't about to confirm her Mummy's fears and just sat looking down at her hands in her lap.

"Can I ask sweet-pea, is there anything unusual about your friend Fanny?" I said and the little girl turned her head into her mother's bosom.

"I don't want to talk to you anymore." She wailed. Erin was shocked by her daughter's reaction, but I offered a reassuring smile as I stood.

"Let's leave it there for today." I said feeling suddenly drained of all energy. "It's ok, I'll let myself out and I will come back tomorrow if that's ok?" Erin looked utterly crestfallen. Apparently, she was hoping for an instant result, but this was going to be far more difficult than I had thought.

18

Normal people can endure low blood sugar levels without transforming into a rabid, irrational beast, but I am not normal people. There had been times in the past when, having been made to wait just twenty minutes longer than the standard dinner schedule on the rare occasion where Ben had offered to cook, I had been reduced to threatening to stab him if he didn't get a move on. I'd come close to being barred from several local restaurants for fixing poor waitresses with my psychotic stare whilst mildly inconvenienced waiting for my meal to arrive, to the dismay of Ben and the girls.

After my morning at The Crown, I was murderously ravenous, so I walked down into town to stock up on biscuits and chocolate before my long trek home. The steep hill at the top of town sapped the final dredges of energy left and the weak muscles in my legs battled with every step. Ben walked alongside me in silence. Even the sound of the church choir practising Christmas Carols at St Lawrence's wasn't enough to lift my spirits. I cast a look left as we walked past the secondary school; Becky and Sophie would be somewhere in the sprawling building hurrying between lessons or milling about in the corridors with their friends. I was slightly ashamed to admit I was jealous of their carefree existence. How glorious would it be to live a life without the tedious worry of bills and putting food on the table. But then, my girls had had to deal with a lot more than I had at their age. I walked on with lead-laden legs, as if I had aged thirty years since I last walked the route a few hours previously. The pavement and road were still littered with golden leaves, mulching down into a slippery mush in the wintery rain.

"Are you ready to talk?" Ben asked. I nodded my head. I wasn't really but we needed to make a start on the case. "About Alex." He added. I stopped walking. I hadn't expected that.

"No, not that. Not now." I managed through a constricted throat.

"Okay, whenever you're ready." He said quietly and I felt him dissipate from my side. His absence registered instantly, and I was surprised by how sad it made me. I managed to shuffle the rest of the way home, head bowed and face set in an empty stare. Resisting the urge to collapse onto my face as soon as I walked through the door, I crawled with my carrier bag of junk food and my coat and shoes still on, upstairs to my bedroom. I woke up several hours later, still fully clothed and under the covers, with the shameful detritus of my sinful snacking spread around me on the duvet. Sophie was sat on the bed looking at me with an exaggerated frown. It's tough being patronised by your own teenage offspring.

"Oh, sorry love." I said struggling to sit up. Every muscle in my body ached. I wondered if this was what it felt like for that strange breed of person that voluntarily undertakes physical exercise. "Have you been home long?"

"It's five o'clock, Mum." She said putting the back of her hand to my forehead like I used to do to her when she was little, "Are you feeling ok?"

"I'm not feeling great if I'm honest." I said and collapsed back onto the pillows. I pulled back the covers in dramatic fashion and attempted to convince my leg to slip out of the bed. "I'll fix us some tea."

"It's fine Mum," she said pulling back the covers over me, "Aunty Immy came round with a Chinese. Do you want me to bring you up some?" Guilt receded, replaced by a wash of relief. Most of my life my sister had been a royal pain in the arse, but sometimes, just sometimes, she turned up at just the right moment and completely saved my bacon.

"I'm okay, but thank you love." I said, "I think I may have inadvertently consumed an entire week's calories in one afternoon." She scanned the room, spotting the rubbish scattered around me and started to pick up the wrappers.

"Don't worry, I'll get rid of the evidence." She said with a cheeky grin. That's my girl. I slipped silently back into my sugar coma and didn't wake again until it was dark. This time it was Ben that was sat on the edge of my bed. I stole the pillows from his side of the bed and used them to prop myself up a little more. I could tell from the soft glow in the hallway that the girls were in bed with their bedside lamps on. I turned my own on and checked the time on my mobile, spotting but ignoring the fact that there was one missed call (from Alex) and three text messages (in all likelihood also from Alex). I felt my cheeks colour and turned the phone, face down on the bed. Ben was sat, looking at his hands which were rested in his ghostly lap.

"You okay?" he said quietly. I nodded.

"I feel like I've been hit by a train, but I'm ok." I said.

"It's the prolonged contact with the spirit world." He said, sounding very much like he'd been doing his homework, "It drains your energy quite quickly if you are doing it a lot in a short space of time. You should build up some stamina after a while. If you do it enough."

"That's good to know." I said, well it kind of was and kind of wasn't, but I would just have to adapt. "Any more news on the case at The Crown?" I was hoping that he had not been idle while I had been recovering.

"I'm trying to keep a low profile, so I don't scare the crap out of that little girl again." His face was sour and I could tell he was mortified about the whole experience, "But I did have a chat with another spirit I found skulking in the basement. He used to be a barman back in the seventies. Died of lung cancer in 1984 he said. He's a funny character, used to do magic tricks for all of the locals apparently. Bit of a local celeb, like your dad. He spent ages going on about how much everything has changed since his time. Got a right bee in his bonnet about the smoking ban. You'd have thought he'd have been a bit more supportive of it but there you go."

"Yeah, I meant any useful news about the haunting at The Crown?" I said. I didn't have the energy to be patient.

"I'm getting to that. This guy I was talking to, Patrick, reckons he's seen the girl with no eyes about a lot. He said she's been talking to Natalie for a while now."

"Tell me something I don't know."

"I'm about to if you give me the chance." He

paused for dramatic effect, all the while my irritation strained to apocalyptic rage, possibly due to the dramatic dip in my blood sugar levels. "So, he was talking about that bar guy, the one with all the metal in his face." Now my interest was piqued and my grumpiness ebbed slightly.

"Go on…"

"Patrick said he saw the guy from the bar down in the basement. He was acting a bit shifty he said so he watched him for a bit to see what he was up to. Patrick said it was a bit weird him standing around in a damp corner as if he was waiting for someone. Then this guy turns up, but he's not a living guy, he's dressed in an old-fashioned suit with a waistcoat. They got talking."

"Wait, he was talking to a spirit?" I said and Ben nodded, "He said he hadn't seen anything! Lying bastard!"

"Well, technically he's not seen anything that's scared him because Patrick said they were talking for ages, like they knew each other pretty well."

"Did he hear what they were talking about?" This seemed relevant somehow, but I wasn't exactly sure how. More than anything I wanted to know why the creepy barman didn't mention this before.

"No, he said he got a bad feeling about the two of them and decided to steer clear."

"Shame. Could have been relevant to the case. Maybe." We both sat quietly considering all the information that we had gathered so far on the case, which it seemed was no further along than it had been before our trip to the inn that day. It was so frustrating; there was a huge sense of urgency, but how could we push it forward. Particularly without pushing a potentially vulnerable little girl to help us. "So, what do we do now?" I asked after a protracted silence in which we both stared at the walls.

"I have to admit I'm feeling more than a tiny bit out of my depth." He said. Despair descended. I'd hoped he would have some answers for me, at the very least an action plan. Ben had always been the one to take the lead and get things sorted. I'd spent my entire adult life relying on him; our chief problem-solver. Suddenly everything seemed utterly bleak and I just wanted to roll over and cry myself to sleep. "We need to get back in there tomorrow. I'll keep an eye on that barman and you see if you can get any more information out of the little girl."

"I just don't understand. If the girl with no eyes is so keen to get us to investigate the haunting, then why doesn't she just tell us what's going on? And why does everything we've learnt so far seem to suggest she's the one behind the haunting?" Ben thought about it for a while.

"Maybe she doesn't want us there to investigate the haunting. Maybe there is something else going on that she needs us to know about?" It seemed so obvious, and I knew straight away that he must be right. Yet instantly I was frustrated again. What did she want us know and why couldn't she just tell us? I was too exhausted to think on it anymore. I needed sleep and judging by how Ben's form was blurring at the edges he needed rest too. He slipped away without another word and I fell into a deep sleep.

19

The next morning, I was up and dressed before the girls for a change. They wandered downstairs, bleary eyed to find me tucking into leftover Chinese takeaway for my breakfast, because I was a grown woman capable of making my own choices and why the hell not? The week had felt like a marathon so far and my body was crying out for sustenance and carbs. I'd woken up with a fire in my belly and a fresh motivation to get the case cracked. If nothing else, it would distract Ben from the Alex question and me from...well Alex and the prospect of an eternity hanging out with my dead husband. I still wasn't sure how much Ben knew or even why he wanted to discuss it with me, but I felt a burning need to kick this can down the road as far and as long as I possibly could. Not that it would achieve anything, but I just needed time for my sluggish brain to come to terms with how things were. Becky and Sophie sat up at the breakfast bar, opposite me, their faces abject revulsion.

"Sustenance." I said through a mouth full of Chow Mein.

"Rank." said Becky with a sneer.

"I've got a busy day." I said and they perked up.

"Oh, have you got a job?" asked Sophie, her

bright blue eyes literally twinkled with enthusiasm and I was reminded of the scared little girl at The Crown Inn.

"Kind of." I said, regretting my boast as now I needed to find a way to explain without really explaining. "I'm a consultant." Becky looked dubious.

"Who are you consulting with and why?" she asked.

"Well..." I made a point of swallowing a mouthful hard to give me time to think, "I'm a management consultant. So, I'm consulting with the managers of The Crown Inn on how to manage better and also the consultative elements within that process in order to...err...facilitate better their management needs in a consultative manner." Nailed it.

"Okay, several of those phrases you just used, are not actual phrases and they didn't make any sense at all." said Becky.

"So, says you." I said thinking myself rather smart. My girls were, however, exceptionally sharp. They were in no way fooled. "Don't worry girls. I've got this covered." They knew me too well to believe that even for a second.

"Keira's dad is a management consultant." Said Sophie. "She says he doesn't know what he does for a living either." Well that's reassuring, I thought. "I'm proud of you Mum." She slipped off the chair and kissed me on the cheek and then wrinkled her nose. "You smell of Chinese." Her sister followed suit, flinging an arm around my neck and pulling me to her for a kiss.

"Yeah, I'd have a breath mint or two before you go, if I were you. Maybe three actually." They both slung their backpacks across one shoulder and headed to the door.

"Bye girls. Have a lovely day. I love you." I called

out before the door slammed behind them.

"There's some extra strong mints in the snack cupboard" said Ben as he appeared in the seat recently vacated by our youngest daughter. I shoveled the remainder of my slutty breakfast hastily into my mouth as he watched with a combination of disgust and fascination.

"Must be weird not being able to eat." I said.

"I'm not hungry."

"Never stopped you before." I grinned.

"I wouldn't be able to taste it and besides I just don't feel like I would want to eat anything, even if I had the necessary physical capability." Eating had always been a big thing for Ben, and never the right kinds of foods either. At home he was constantly in the snack cupboard or pestering for a takeaway, even when me and the girls were sick of the greasy dinners. God only knows what he had eaten while he was on the go at work. I suspected his credit card, the one I only found out about when he died, had been used exclusively for McDonalds, chips and grubby service station sandwiches. Yet, to look at him you would never have known he had the diet of an unsupervised toddler at a birthday buffet. His internal organs however, I had been told, were coated in thick layers of fat. We just thought he was lucky with his metabolism and he'd get away with it forever. It was surprisingly devastating to realise that your loved one was actually a ticking time bomb and think about all of the things I did to help him on his way. All the greasy, Saturday morning fry-ups and cupboards full of biscuits and chocolate.

"All set for today?" I asked him.

"Think so. I've been trying to keep an eye on the barman..."

"His name is Robin." I said popping a couple of mints into my mouth.

"Right, well he's spending quite a lot of time at the inn I've noticed. Which is odd given they are not actually open. I'm wondering if he's staying in one of the rooms. Can you ask Erin?"

"Does it make a difference if he is?" I asked.

"I don't know, but I do think we need to establish all of the facts. Something that seems pretty insignificant could be an important clue to what's going on. I think you need to really drill Erin and Matt and if you can get her to talk, Natalie." He was starting to sound like a detective in a cop drama.

"Ok, chief." I gave him a cheeky salute. "Anything in particular you think I should be asking about?"

"Just rely on your instincts and intuition."

"Oh, that's really bloody helpful." I said slipping into my trainers. I was preparing to be at the inn for most of the day, so I was in my jeans and a warm jumper combo. The place was full of draughts and cold spots, but I needed to feel relatively comfortable to get some work done. "Ready?" I said grabbing my bag.

"Ready." He said and he disappeared.

"Oh, I'll walk by myself then." I grumbled heading for the door.

I took a step into the fresh air and drew in a deep breath. The sky was bright and blue, and the sun was shining so hard it hurt my eyes. Despite that it was chillingly cold, so I dashed back indoors to grab my winter coat. I still had to walk fast to keep my extremities from contracting frostbite and falling off. By the time I arrived at the back entrance of the pub, I couldn't feel my own face. I knocked urgently at the door. When Erin finally appeared to let me in, I noticed her eyes were sagging with exhaustion, with thick black circles underneath.

"Oh wow, you look absolutely shattered!" I said as I stepped into what would eventually serve as the hotel's reception area.

"Sorry, we've had a rough night. Come into the bar, I'll make us a coffee and tell you what's been going on." I followed her through a swing door and short corridor into the empty bar at the front of the building. There was no sign of Matt or Robin, but Natalie was sat on a tall stool at the bar colouring in.

"Oh, hello." I said trying too hard to sound super friendly. She looked up at me. She too looked exhausted, but still managed a gallant attempt at a smile.

"Hello." she said in a tiny voice. I wanted to grab her and give her a big hug and tell her that everything was going to be ok, but I couldn't. Besides the fact she might find my behaviour a bit creepy, I didn't know if everything was actually going to be ok so instead, I hefted myself onto a bar stood, using the bar to steady myself.

"What are you colouring?" I asked.

"It's a Uni-Pug." She answered in a matter-of-fact tone.

"A Uni-what?" I looked closer at the picture of what appeared to be a rainbow coloured dog with a horn between its eyes. "Oh, I see." I said. I didn't see. I was eternally grateful that my daughters were too old to get caught up in the unicorn mania. All those lurid colours made me feel a little bit queasy. "It is lovely." I added just as Erin returned with two mugs of steaming coffee. She sipped hers and smiled a wide, generous grin.

"That's better. At least, it might get me through the morning anyway." She stayed behind the bar, leaning her head against one of the beer pumps with her eyes closed, her mahogany hair draped over one shoulder. Now there's a hard-working mum, who desperately needs a break I thought. I took my own cup in my hands and let the warmth start to thaw my fingers. It smelt divine.

"So, what's been going on?" I said.

"It's been a rough night." Erin said with a lung draining sigh. "It started off okay, but we just had this feeling like there was this energy building in the place. You know, like something was about to happen. Even Robin was a bit spooked."

"Is he planning on staying here long?" I asked jumping on the opportunity, perhaps a little prematurely. It wasn't terribly unusual for staff to live on site in the hospitality industry, but when the owner and their family were also living on site it seemed a bit of a weird set up to me.

"We're not sure how long he's staying. He was at a bit of a loose end and what with all these empty rooms, seemed churlish not to let him stay, until he gets back on his feet. I don't really know what's going on, he spoke to Matt about it, but I think he split up with a girlfriend or something. Anyway, it's nice to have more people about, rather than rattling around in this big old building by ourselves. I just wish he wouldn't stay up with Matt drinking all of our profits, you know?" She looked peeved and stopped to take another sip of coffee. I wasn't sure how she could drink it already, mine was like molten lava, despite the chill in the room. "Why, do you ask?" she said suddenly.

"I'm just trying to establish the situation here and any recent changes in circumstances. Anything really that might contribute to the occurrences that you have reported. Robin mentioned yesterday that he hadn't experienced anything strange while he has been here. Do you find that a bit strange? That he is the only one." I noticed as I was speaking that Natalie had stopped colouring in and was frozen, listening intently to every word we were saying. Erin had noticed too.

"Natalie love, why don't you go give your Dad a nudge and see if he's awake." Erin leaned across the bar and stroked her daughter's cheek as she spoke to her.

"Ok Mummy." She said clambering off her barstool with some skill and more agility that I knew I would manage when I attempted the same. She skipped through the bar and out the door.

"Sorry, where were we?" asked Erin. "Oh yes, Robin. No, I don't think it's strange. He's a very down to earth young man. I think he's just quite closed off to stuff like that. He just doesn't believe so he doesn't see what everyone else has been seeing." I knew otherwise so I wasn't buying it, but I didn't let on to Erin.

"So, tell me about last night."

"Everything was fine at first. We got Natalie to bed as normal and I was upstairs in the flat watching shite on the tv while Matt was down at the bar with Robin. It seems to be all he wants to do at the moment. He's not coping with how badly things are going for us." She looked aggravated. It couldn't be easy to admit all of this to a practical stranger, but at the same time I thought she must be too tired to keep her guard up. "I'd just fallen asleep on the couch waiting for Matt to come up when I heard noises coming from the other end of the flat, near Natalie's room. I ran out to see what was going on. Robin and Matt were already in Natalie's room. They said they'd heard noises and were checking that everything was ok. Thankfully, Natalie was still fast asleep at that point. I managed to convince Matt to come to bed with me and Rob headed off to his room. Couldn't have been more than half an hour later when there was an almighty racket from the floor below. We ran down to find all of the doors to the hotel rooms, being slammed shut. They'd fly open seconds later and slam hard again. It went on for about five minutes, all these doors slamming and opening and slamming again. I was terrified one of the neighbours was going call the police. Natalie came down crying her eyes out. Poor thing was petrified. When it finally stopped, Robin came out of his room looking a bit shaken and I was thinking, oh great, now he's going to leave, but he was laughing it off after a little while. We did ask him if he wanted to come upstairs to sleep in the flat on the sofa, but he said he was fine and went back to bed. Natalie slept in our bed for the rest of the night. It took me forever to get back to sleep. You know when you just get this feeling that something is about to happen and you're just on edge? I was like that all night. I think I finally got to sleep about three am but I must have woken up every ten minutes. I feel like I've hardly slept at all."

When she finished talking, she took a deep slurp of her coffee and I tried to think of anything I could possibly say that might be reassuring. This was why paranormal investigations should not be left to the amateurs but for some reason, Ben and I had been dragged into this situation. My attention was suddenly distracted by a large black dog that sauntered across from the back bar, across to the empty fireplace. He looked like some kind of shaggy greyhound but with thick black fur. He collapsed on the hearthstone with a satisfied grunt.

"I didn't know you had a dog." I turned to Erin who was watching me curiously.

"I don't." She said and I looked to the fireplace. Erin did the same and then we looked back at each other. I pointed over at the creature and she looked again and looked back at me.

"There's nothing there." She said. I looked back yet again, and the hound yawned. I looked back to Erin wide eyed with a definitive shiver. Oh crap, I thought, I'm seeing them all now.

20

We were climbing the stairs up to the first floor, as Robin was coming down. Despite the dark circles under his eyes, there was a bounce in his step as he practically skipped down to the bar with the hint of a smile on his face. He still made my skin crawl, although I couldn't place exactly why. Those impenetrable dark eyes were unsettling and seemed to mock me.

"Hey Rob," said Erin stopping mid-step, "Tracey just met our resident ghost hound." Robin brightened and a full grin spread to the piercings in each cheek, which served to create dimples. I wondered if they were joined with a bar across his mouth, like a horse's bit.

"Hope he didn't scare you too much?" he said with a snigger.

"Not at all." I replied, hoping he would spot the ice in my smile, "Nothing I can't handle anyway. Thought you didn't believe in all this stuff anyway?"

"I don't. It's all nonsense." He said with a shrug and carried on down the stairs.

Erin and I continued up to the first floor. The landing was dark; there were no windows, only half a dozen doors to the hotel rooms, all of which were closed. Erin pulled out a huge bunch of keys and flicked through the numbers until she got the key for the first door.

"Did you lock them all after last night's shenanigans?" I asked.

"Nope," she said unlocking the door, "I locked them before last night's shenanigans."

"Oh." My extensive google based research told me this was one powerful poltergeist, with the power to lock and unlock doors, although I decided not to share this revelation with Erin.

The first room was not much lighter than the corridor we had just left. The day was rapidly turning into the kind where I should have been at home, wearing my favourite woolly jumper, curled up in front of the fire with a nice cup of tea and a good book. The rain clouds had rolled in from nowhere and shrouded everything in grey. The room was freezing and I pulled my cardigan close around me.

"Sorry, we've turned the radiators off in all the rooms in anticipation of an epic gas bill."

"That's ok," I said pacing around the room, attempting to create the majestic air of a medium tuning in with the spirit world. I went as far as to close my eyes and put out the feelers on all of my senses. The room fell silent.

"Whatca doin?" asked Ben. I opened one eye a slit to find him watching me curiously. I hoped that the look I was giving him back adequately conveyed my 'piss off I'm trying to attune' vibe. He cocked his head like a confused puppy, and I abandoned my efforts.

"I'm not picking up on anything in here." I said. "Perhaps, if you wouldn't mind, I could have a wander around the place and just see what I can pick up on?"

"Oh sure," Erin handed me the keys, "although,

if you wouldn't mind staying out of room twenty-three. That's where Robin is staying. I'm sure he wouldn't mind you going in there, but if you could just ask him first please." She gave me a tired smile and left the room. I stayed silent until I heard her footsteps heading up to the second floor.

"Well?" I asked Ben and he looked taken aback. "Robin? Have you been watching him? Were you here last night? Apparently, it kicked off, big time."

"I wasn't here last night, and I've only been here as long as you have so I haven't had much of a chance to keep an eye on him."

"So, what are you doing here talking to me?" I was getting a bit impatient with him. They do say working with your partner is never a good idea. At least I knew we couldn't get a divorce.

"Sorry. Just wanted to check you were ok. And..." he hesitated.

"And what...?"

"There's a fuck off great big dog down in the bar where Robin is and it won't go away." Ben had always had a morbid fear of dogs, especially big ones. He'd once told me that he'd nearly been mauled by a bull mastiff when he was very young, perhaps two or three years old. The owner had managed to pull the dog off him before it had done too much damage, but it had still scratched his face pretty bad. He still had the faintest silvery scars on the side of his face into adulthood. Any attempts to grow a beard had left him with ridges of bald patches running from his chin to the corner of his mouth.

Not knowing what else to do and impatient to get on with the job, I whistled loud. Soon after we heard large dog lumbering up the stairs.

"Thanks." Ben said and disappeared.

I lingered in the hotel rooms a short while longer, but I struggled to sense anything more than the panting dog which seemed to have decided to follow me everywhere, padding ahead of me as I entered each room and collapsing in a heap in the middle of the floor. Unlike Ben, I had always loved dogs and this one was a particularly good boy. I had to fight the urge to put my hand out to pat his head, knowing that my hand would just pass through the spectral pooch.

Finally, I headed up the stairs to the next floor. I wanted to find Erin first to check she didn't mind me coming up to their private flat, but I found her laying face first on the sofa snoring gently and I didn't have the heart to wake her. I withdrew from the room and pulled the door slightly to. From the end of the corridor I could hear Natalie's voice. I moved closer to hear what she was saying, imagining that she was making her dolls talk to one another, like Sophie and Becky used to before they turned into raging, stroppy teenagers.

"This one is called Molly." She was saying in a whispered voice, but I could tell she was smiling as she said it. "No not that one, he's in time out for flashing his bum at the teacher." She giggled, but then I heard a sound that made my blood freeze. It was a deep rasping noise, but unmistakably another voice replying to her. I couldn't make out the words, but the voice injected pure terror into me. I didn't want to, but I moved closer, feeling the temperature edge down by degrees the closer I got along the shady corridor. Not wanting to scare Natalie, I crept to the crack in the door edge and peeked into the room. On the floor sat cross legged was Natalie, dressed in fleece pajamas with dolls laid across her lap and a big smile on her chubby little face.

Another girl sat opposite, with her back to me. Her long dark hair hung limp down her back, and she was wearing a navy-blue dress, tucked neatly under her. While my brain struggled to process what I was seeing, the girls fell silent. I heard one of them making a shushing noise and the other girl started to turn her head. I couldn't bear to see her, because I knew instinctively this was the girl with no eyes. I ducked out of sight. The hushed voices continued and then I heard the sound of gentle footsteps approaching. I was panting softly trying to get the thunder of my heartbeat under control with my back against the wall, when Natalie poked her head out into the corridor. I almost swore with relief.

"Hello." She said shyly.

"Hello sweetpea," I was slightly breathless, but I could feel the temperature creeping back up, so I knew the girl with no eyes had gone. "What are you playing?"

"I was just showing Fanny my favourite toys." She said looking back into the room, "Oh! She's gone." She looked a little sad. I thought it must be tough being an only child.

"Ah...that's a shame. I was hoping to meet your new friend." I lied. "Does she disappear like that a lot." I asked and Natalie just shrugged as little girls are wont to do. She padded back into her room and sat back down on the floor cross legged and picked up on of her dolls.

"Tell me, have you met the dog?" I asked and her face lit up with a dazzling smile and she nodded up at me. Feeling like we'd broken the ice, I ventured a little into the room and knelt opposite her. The floor still felt stone cold from its previous occupant. "Do you know if he has a name? He really is a magnificent doggo." I could hear the gentle thud of his tail wagging against the wall in the hallway where he was laid.

"I don't think he has a name." She said and then gasped. "Can I give him a name?" Her eyes were practically effervescent with excitement.

"Oh definitely, he needs a name!" The tail thudding against the wall grew louder and I laughed, pointing out into the corridor I asked, "Can you hear that?" Natalie giggled behind her hand and nodded.

"I think..." she screwed up her face in concentration, "I think he's a Bert." I couldn't help but laugh.

"Bert is a fantastic name." I thought to myself, this child is just pure joy. It had been such a long time since I had smiled so much, and it was a lovely feeling. The corners of my mouth positively ached, but then I remembered I was there to do a job and the smile slowly slid away. I watched Natalie fussing over her dolls for a moment, thinking about how best to approach my next question.

"So, tell me about your friend, Fanny." I blurted it out, "Is there anything unusual about her?" Natalie barely looked up from her dolls and I took this as a sign she trusted me.

"Her dress is a bit funny." She said.

"Oh. How is it funny?"

"I don't know." She screwed up her nose for a second deep in thought. "I like it though. It's pretty. It's like my other doll Samantha." She stood and walked over to toy chest. Carefully lifting the top, she knelt in front of it and dug around until she pulled out a small doll with a plastic face and long nylon blond hair. Her dress was a high necked, frilly affair; unmistakably Victorian in style.

"Oh, that's interesting." I considered digging further as she unceremoniously flung the doll back in the chest and returned to her position on the floor. "And what does she look like? I mean like her face?"

"She's pretty. She's got long brown hair and freckles." But her eyes, I thought desperately, what about her eyes? Natalie looked up and met my eye in a way I found slightly unnerving. "She has light blue eyes, like the colour of the sky on a sunny day." Then she smiled and picked up her dolls again. I took this to mean our conversation was over and she had lost interest in me.

"Okay sweetpea," I said when I'd digested this new information. "I'll leave you to play." She ignored me as I stood up and silently left the room. I instructed Bert to stay and called him a good boy before heading towards the stairs down to the pub. I got halfway down the corridor before I heard Natalie's hushed voice and Fanny's rasping reply.

21

Ben's spirit jumped up from where it had been "sitting" and peered behind me nervously as I stepped into the bar. I rolled my eyes and he relaxed a little when he realised the hound was not with me. Matt was sat on a bar stool and Robin was behind the bar pouring them both a pint. They both stopped talking when I entered the room. I couldn't help but look at my watch. It was barely ten thirty and my stomach churned. Offering them a tight smile, that was largely ignored, I walked past them to the door that led down to the basement.

"Don't mind me gents." I said as I swept past them. They didn't, although I sensed a teeny bit of hostility, particularly from Robin, whose dark eyes followed me intently. I hoped that Ben would follow my cue and meet me in the cellar. When I arrived in the damp little room it was empty, except for me and I hefted myself onto a high stool while I waited impatiently for my late husband to pitch up. The bottom of the window ledge sat neatly on the high street pavement and I could hear heavy footsteps rushing past the window and the hum of traffic charging down the high street. I wondered for a moment if I should go back up and get him, when Ben finally appeared.

"Sorry." He said, "I just wanted to see if they said anything about you after you'd gone."

"Good idea. Did they?"

"Nah, but they definitely aren't happy about you being here."

"Could've fooled me." I snorted. "So, any news?"

"They both seem pretty unsettled about last night, so I'm guessing they are just as in the dark as we are." It hurt to admit it, but he was right. Our progress was painfully slow. "How about you?" Ben asked.

"I've just seen the girl with no eyes, well...I thought I had. Natalie's friend Fanny. I just caught them in Natalie's room. I was convinced that Fanny was the girl with no eyes, but I managed to get Natalie to describe her to me and she didn't mention anything about her eyes except they are blue."

"Oh, so definitely not the girl with no eyes?"

"I'm not convinced." I said, "Can you not make contact with her again?" Ben took a step back.

"Do I have to?"

"No, but I think it would really help." I hated asking him to do something he really didn't want to do, but it felt as though we had hit a brick wall with our investigation, and I was running out of options. "Are there any other spirits here we could talk to?" Ben stood very still, as if deep in concentration. Ben's form shimmered and I worried he was going to disappear altogether. I felt a shift in the air around us; it had grown heavier, denser. The room seemed to quiver as shapes formed out of the gloom. The space around us started to fill with spiritual forms, until we were surrounded, and the tiny basement felt crowded and uncomfortable. To my right a wiry man in tight jeans and Rolling Stones tee-shirt greeted Ben like an old friend, grasping his hand and shaking it vigorously. A small boy in filthy ripped clothes, crept amongst the adults and fished through pockets on the scrounge, before dodging back through the crowd. A young girl in a low-cut top was rubbing herself shamelessly against a ramrod straight gent in tailcoats and a top hat. His face coloured as he struggled to mumble in response. A woman appeared to my left. She was laced into an impossibly tight corset dress, with deeply rouged cheeks and badly drawn on eyebrows, giving her a look of perpetual puzzlement.

"She's a rough one that lass." She slurred in a thick country accent. "Shameless!" She tutted and made an attempt at raising both eyebrows, which just elevated the look of confused bemusement a little further.

"Yeah!" I said attempting to establish some common ground, "So, do you know anything about the girl with no eyes?" I dove straight in. She seemed a little taken aback at first and took a moment to compose herself.

"A girl with no eyes you says?" she thought hard, attempting to furrow her brow. Her eyebrows were in all out rebellion now and there was no discerning what she was thinking from her face. "I don't think I know no girl with no eyes. Ey, Mary!" she called across the room at a large framed lady in a long flowing dress, her brown hair pulled tight back from her pudgy face. "You know anything about a girl with no eyes?" Her friend made a concerted effort to consider this, I knew this because she pulled her chin right back into her other chin and went slightly cross-eyed.

"No," she said in an unusually deep voice for a

woman, "Don't fink I does, Jane. A girl with no eyes you says? Tha's a bit weird in't it!" she laughed heartily. Both women looked at me. I could tell they were desperate to help, but I suspected they might lack the capacity to be any real help me.

"Okay, well thank you very much for your help anyway." I said trying to extricate myself. They looked a little crestfallen.

"Ere, are you the lady what's been brought in to figure out why all the weird stuff's been going on?" Mary asked enthusiastically, with a smile so wide it showed all of her teeth...all three of them.

"Well, yes. I am trying." I said and they laughed and clapped with delight.

"Oi John!" howled Ann, "You know anything about a girl what's got no eyes?"

"No eyes?" declared a rotund man appearing out of the melee. He was tall with thick black hair swept across a thinning scalp. His eyes were a piercing dark blue and he stared me down with a scrutiny that was intimidating. "No, I can't say that I have. Why, the only little girl we have here is little Fanny."

"Oh, little Fanny is a right sweetheart!" declared Ann grasping her hands to her bosom and smiling sweetly.

"Oh, that she be!" nodded Mary in agreement. "That she be." My interest was piqued.

"Is Fanny here by any chance?" I asked looking around the room eagerly for a small figure that might be obscured by the other ghostly bodies filling the room. Mary, Ann and John all look around. Mary looked behind herself and then lifted her voluminous skirts to check between her pale chubby thighs before looking at me and shrugging.

"She doesn't seem to be. Why are you asking after her?" asked John.

"I'm investigating some disturbances that have been going on and I wondered if Fanny might know anything about what has been going on." I asked. The idiot brigade fell silent and looked to one another in a conspiratorial way. "Do you happen to know anything that might help me?" I asked. They all mumbled to the negative and started to look a bit shifty. "Okay, well can you tell me anything more about Fanny?" I asked. Infuriatingly they all remained silent, sharing a look between them that seemed to suggest they were not sure if they should say anything or not.

"Not much to say about our Fanny. She's a sweet little thing." Repeated Ann.

"Yes, you already mentioned that." I was gritting my teeth. "Can you tell me why she passed over at such a young age?" I tried to phrase it sensitively, but they prickled immediately. John's face darkened and he stepped closer.

"Now, don't you be bothering yourself with things like that lady." Jane and Mary took a step back and several other spirits stopped their own conversations and turned to look at us.

"I'm sorry I didn't mean to upset anyone. I'm just trying to establish any facts that might be relevant to the case." I said taking a little step back myself. John's spirit seemed to have grown a little and was towering over me.

"I don't think I like your line of questioning. You're making assumptions about our girl and I don't like it." He growled at me. I looked frantically to Ben, who extracted himself from his chat with Patrick and moved in front of me attempting to deflect John's anger. Something seemed to pass between them, like unspoken words and John's spirit seemed to shrink slightly. His face softened and I started to feel my panic ebb a little. In the periphery of my vision I could see the other spirits in the room start to fade. John shot a warning look over Ben's shoulder at me and then turned and walked into a wall. Only Mary and Ann remained of the spirits in the basement with Ben and I. Ann stepped forward shyly.

"It's dreadful what he done to that girl," she said quietly, looking around to check John hadn't reappeared.

"Who? Did someone do something to Fanny?" I asked urgently. They were starting to fade.

"It was Freddie what done it." Sobbed Mary, and the two women embraced.

"Just too dreadful." Said Ann and they turned and walked away, dissipating into thin air, leaving just Ben and I alone in the basement. I felt my stomach lurch as I finally realised what my instincts have been shouting at me all along.

"Fanny is the girl with no eyes." I said to Ben. "We need to speak to her right now."

22

I could hear raised voices as I climbed the stairs back into the bar. I stopped and listened at the door.

"What were you doing in her room?" Matt's voice was slurred but clearly angry. Robin's by contrast was calm, flippant even.

"I heard a noise. I was just checking she was okay."

"If I catch you near her..." he slurred off, his threat faltering as if he was falling asleep. Then there was silence. I had asked Ben to go "track down Fanny", and when he had finished giggling like a little girl, he had done just that. I just needed to slip upstairs and let Erin know I was heading back home. I was making progress but every encounter with spirits sapped my energy and right then I just needed to regroup and assimilate the scant information that we had.

Tentatively, I pushed open the door and peered into the bar. As I suspected, Matt was asleep at the bar, his head rested in the crook of his elbow. Robin had gone. I crept through the bar, heading through the door leading up to the first floor. Treading softly, I was listening all the while. Turning into the corridor where the hotel rooms were, light was flooding out of the open door to Robin's room. I edged closer and listened carefully. A rogue floorboard creaked under my foot and I heard a shuffling from the room. Robin appeared seconds later. He glared at me and pulled the door shut, but not before I spotted the figure of a man dressed in a black suit stood in the corner of the room. His eyes were venomous slits and his lip snarled up in a scowl. I shuddered and turned.

In the living room Erin was still comatose on the sofa. I checked her breathing, because I'm a pessimist like that, and drew a blanket over her. Poking my head around Natalie's room I found her reading a book on her bed, her knees drawn up to rest the book on and a doll tucked tight into her arm. Natalie gripped the head of the doll casting its view right and left across the pages.

"Hey sweetpea," I said. I wasn't sure it was wise for me to leave her unsupervised, with both parents out for the count so I decided to stick around a little longer. "Have you had any lunch?" I asked. She shook her head, making her soft blond fringe bounce across her forehead. I took her hand and we headed to the kitchen. Perhaps I should add childminding to the list of services on my website, I thought.

The kitchen was ridiculously small with a single window over the sink and units crowded along two of the walls in an L shape. A wide pine table domineering the centre made it difficult to manoeuvre around the room without bumping into sideboards or walls.

"What do you fancy?" I turned to her as she slipped onto a chair.

"Ice cream!" she yelled with delight. Concentrating hard on producing a sincere frown, I looked down at the little girl with my hands on my hips, but I had to fight off a smirk that threatened to curl at the corners of my lips.

"That doesn't sound like a healthy, nutritious lunch for a growing girl!" She just shrugged and smiled up at me hopefully. "Fair enough." I said reaching down to the freezer. "Hmmm...chocolate or strawberry?"

"Both!" she giggled, and I laughed. God loves a tryer. I hunted around for a bowl and plopped a scoop of each flavour into it. Natalie reached out eagerly for the bowl as I handed it to her and I sat opposite her at the table. She tucked in, savouring the treat and I smiled. In that moment, I was reminded so much of my girls when they were her age. Teenage girls were phenomenal hard work, even when they were sweethearts like my two, but the hardest part was when they just didn't want to spend time with their dear old ma anymore. I desperately missed the long chats and cuddles and sitting cross legged on the living room floor playing board games and just the general being needed by my children. They'd grown up so much in such a short time and I was dismayed that they had inherited Ben's need to be fiercely independent.

"Oh, hello Fanny." Said Natalie so suddenly, every hair on my body leapt up on end. I turned my head slowly. The little girl was stood in the corner of the kitchen. Her long dark hair hung in clumps down her slim shoulders. Her skin was deathly pale, and her hands swung limply by her side. Her face was turned down so I couldn't see her eyes, but I was more certain than ever. The girl with no eyes was Fanny.

"Come sit next to me." said Natalie. Fanny shifted across the room and settled in the seat. I couldn't fathom how little Natalie could not be unsettled by the sight of this dark brooding little girl as I sat frozen with terror.

Fanny started to turn her head up. Oh god no, I thought. I didn't want Natalie to see how I reacted to her, but I was helpless to move. As her head lifted, deliberately slowly the spirit lightened. Suddenly her hair was no longer dark and limp, but a light mousy brown and clean and thick, hanging in two neat plaits on her shoulders. Her dress was transformed from a murky dark blue, into a light blue pattern, swirling with birds and feathers and a pristine white collar. As her face turned up to mine, I saw a clear faced young girl with a small pouting pink mouth and deep cornflower blue eyes. A smattering of freckles across her nose reminded me of Natalie and my own little Becky. I realised for the first time that this was just a tragic young girl whose life had ended far too soon. My heart ached with sadness for her.

"I've got ice cream!" announced Natalie to her friend and Fanny peered into the bowl. She looked in wonder at the brightly coloured slush and licked her lips. I didn't want to interfere in this little moment between the two friends, so I just sat back in my chair and watched them.

"I've never had ice cream." No longer a deep and rasping noise, Fanny's voice was soft and quiet.

"What? No way! Here try some." said Natalie and she held up a dripping spoon. Fanny grinned and opened her mouth. The spoon went in and came straight back out again still covered in ice cream. Fanny patted her stomach in exaggerated style and the girls collapsed in giggles. A shuffling noise in the corridor stole our attention and we turned to see a dishevelled Erin shuffling into the kitchen, yawning widely before shivering in her thick cardigan. I looked back and saw Fanny had disappeared.

"Ice cream?" Erin said with a raised eyebrow and the hint of a smile.

"Sorry," I said sheepishly, "She told me you always let her have ice cream for lunch." Natalie proper belly-laughed.

"Oh, did she now?" Erin laughed too, "Cheeky little monkey!" She tickled her daughter, then lifted her out of the chair, sitting down herself and placing the little girl on her lap. Natalie leaned forward to finish shovelling the ice cream into her mouth.

"Feeling any better?" I asked and she groaned.

"A little but I could do with another five hours of sleep." My lopsided smile of motherly solidarity did little to console her, but I sensed she appreciated the gesture anyway. "Any news? On the...you know?"

"We are making progress. I am in contact with the spirit behind the occurrences, but I'm still trying to understand her motives. I'm afraid it might take a little more time, but I assure you I am doing everything that I can." She was nodding as I spoke. I wished I could offer her more concrete reassurances, but I couldn't do it to the poor woman. She was already dead on her feet. "Can I ask, how did you come across Robin?" Mildly heffalumpish in delivery, I thought, and I winced as Erin reacted by stiffening in her seat.

"Go play in your room," she whispered into Natalie's ear as the little girl finished licking her bowl clean and she kissed the side of her forehead. She continued once Natalie was out of earshot. "Why do you ask?" she said impatiently.

"I just wanted to get all of the background information I can. It could be helpful if the disturbances started when one person arrived, the spirit..."

"We've already been through this. It's nothing to do with Robin." She said sternly, her tired eyes trained on me. "We hired him about two weeks after we moved in and he's been an absolute rock. The crazy stuff started happening about a month before he had even moved in. So, I think you are barking up the wrong tree there." It was hard to fathom why this young mum, up to her eyeballs in debt, struggling to get a business off the ground and with an alcoholic husband was trying so hard to defend a young man she barely knew. Suddenly I felt both suspicious and a tiny bit angry at Erin. Even if there wasn't something going on between her and Robin, she was being purposefully obstructive in my investigation. She either wanted my help or she didn't. And if she didn't, she needed to stop wasting my time.

"Right, well. I think I've done everything that I can for one day." I stood getting ready to leave. "I'm going to head home. I'll come back in a couple days. Let me know in the meantime if there are any further disturbances." I charged out of the kitchen before she had the chance to respond. I hoped that my anger resonated strongly enough for her to feel it and come to her senses. It felt like we were running out of time.

Stepping out into the murky afternoon, I realised that it was actually warmer outside in the elements than it was inside The Crown Inn. Nevertheless, ice cold drizzle snaked down the nape of my coat, which I wrapped around myself a little tighter as I walked. I'd barely made it as far as the church when I heard my name being called. I turned to see Alex hurrying across the road towards me and my heart lurched.

"So, who's your friend?" said Ben with a teasing smile, appearing suddenly beside me.

"Hi." Said Alex. He seemed to register the shock on my face. "How are you doing?" he looked concerned and uncomfortable, glancing around us.

"Yep, I'm fine. Absolutely fine. Just on my way home actually." I made to turn and head home.

"Don't go." Said Alex reaching out to touch my arm. "Why have you been ignoring my messages?" he looked unbearably sad and I felt wretched. I looked to Ben, who was waiting for me to respond. It took him a moment to realise.

"Oh shit." He said. "This is Alex? Crap sorry. I'll let you guys have a chat." And before I could explain, Ben disappeared. It dawned on me that the conversation I had been trying so hard to avoid was no longer necessary. My deceased husband knew about my infidelity.

23

Alex insisted on walking me home, but we got as far as the junction to my road and he suggested a detour. Steering me in the opposite direction, we crossed to the other side of the road and through a wooden lychgate. I was so caught up in my churning thoughts, I barely registered that we were in a graveyard until we were halfway down the path. The stone epitaphs scattered all around us were a dead giveaway. I stopped. Alex took a moment to notice I wasn't walking along-side him anymore before he turned back.

"You ok?" he took a few steps back towards me. I was looking wildly around me, the last thing I needed right then was to be harangued by a cemetery full of spirits. Thankfully, there didn't appear to be anything living or dead moving amongst the grey stones, apart from a few frantic squirrels bounding manically across the grass.

"Yeah, I'm fine." I said and I stepped forward to catch up with him.

"Shit sorry, poor choice of venue for a walk I guess." I nodded and then shrugged.

"There's no one here I think, so I should be ok." We walked on in silence for a while. Raindrops so cold I was surprised it wasn't actually snowing, splatted on our heads as we followed the overgrown path to the edge of the graveyard and then turned left, walking over the grass that ran adjacent to the cemetery wall. The gravestones there were the oldest and their weathered faces were so worn, they could no longer be read.

"So, how's Ben?" Alex asked eventually. It was a question he had asked a million times in the past, but now that Ben was dead it seemed a little perverse.

"Still dead." I said. "He's helping me with a project."

"Oh?" Alex looked intrigued. "How so?"

"There's been a haunting, a pretty nasty from what I can tell, at The Crown Inn. We're trying to resolve it for the owners." He looked taken aback and more than a little impressed. I had expected him to have been bemused, perhaps take the micky out of me a little, and then I had realised that this was Alex and not my husband. His faith in me was unwavering, if unprecedented.

"Sounds interesting." I could see him looking at me in the corner of my eye, as we walked along. He had a curious way of making me feel like the most beautiful, intelligent and interesting woman on the planet when we were together. I didn't want our first kiss to be there and then and I didn't think I could trust myself not to grab him, so I just kept staring at the wet grass in front of me.

"We don't really know what's going on yet, but we've made contact with the ghost that has been causing all the grief. Well, we think so anyway. It's a bit of a sad story really. She's only a little girl. I think she was murdered."

"That's sad." As he said it, I caught sight of a name on a gravestone and I stopped walking. The grave sat alone in the centre of a large green in the middle of the graveyard. The stone was suspiciously clear and smooth, and the black lettering appeared fresh as if it had been renewed not very long ago. Next to the headstone, a colourful windmill has been planted in the earth and was swirling around in the breeze. We headed in its direction.

"I hate to ask…" he said stopping me on the path and looking down at me. I stopped reluctantly and looked back up at him. I felt naked under the intensity of his stare, but not in an unpleasant way. I knew he liked what he saw, his light green eyes shone, and I could have sworn I could see his pupils dilating. "What's going to happen now?" My old anxiety, an ache in the pit of my stomach returned with such ferocity I thought I might actually be sick.

"I don't know." I frowned and looked down to avoid seeing his face crumple in disappointment. "I just don't know, I'm sorry Alex."

"It's okay, really don't worry. I'm sorry I don't want to push you, I just…" he trailed off.

"What feasible option do we have? It's not like I can move you into the family home. I mean Ben's been a lot more laid back since he's been spirit-side, but I think that might be pushing my luck a little." I smiled up at him, hoping he would meet my eye but he was staring off into the distance, eyes fixed on the spire of the church rising over the edge of the cemetery wall.

I was taken back to the day Ben died, Alex had that same tight jawed look on his face, his eyes wet with tears he was fighting to keep back and not able to look at me. I was doused by a familiar old shame that had haunted me since that day. When I'd gotten the call from Ben's work to tell me my husband had been taken away in an ambulance, I had been stood in the foyer of the Swan hotel. Alex and I had been on the verge of taking our relationship to a new level, we both knew it although it had always gone unspoken. Then my mobile had rung. Alex had to hold me up by the arms as it had been explained to me that my husband was in a critical condition. Even then I hadn't quite comprehended the seriousness of what was happening. I mean, men in their early forties don't just drop dead. I'd played it down as I explained to Alex that I would have to go. His expectations for the day had been so strong he'd leant in for a kiss, but I'd pushed him back. I couldn't share our first kiss knowing that Ben was in hospital, it felt all wrong. Alex, ever the gentleman, had apologised profusely seeming genuinely mortified by his own behaviour, but in the silence that followed he had looked away from me, staring off into the distance battling with his own emotions. To my shame, I'd thought it was over and had left him without another word, silently cursing Ben all the way home for his crappy timing. If only I'd known.

"There's no rush." Alex said when he was finally able to look at me again. "I'll wait as long as it takes until you are ready. I can't walk away from this." I stepped forward, closing the small gap between us and rest my head on his chest. He pulled me into an eager embrace.

"It still hurts." I said resting my chin on his chest and looking up at him, "It's like a gaping space in my chest, where part of my heart has been damaged and it will never be the same." I could tell from his face that he didn't need to be hearing my heartache over the death of my husband, but he needed to know this. "I don't know how much of it was guilt over everything we did."

"We didn't do anything, not really." I shook my head. It didn't make any difference if there had been no physical relationship, it was still a betrayal.

"It doesn't matter, but anyway, the guilt was only part of the pain. There was just this god-awful feeling, when something you can't change happens. It doesn't matter how much you plead with the universe for this to not be happening to you. You'd give anything for this to not be happening to you and it's like the gates of hell have opened up underneath your feet and there absolutely nothing that you can do."

"I don't understand. You always said that you were unhappy with him. All those rotten things he said to you were making you miserable."

"I still loved him, Alex." My eyes pleaded with him not to step away but he still did and the cold of the air around us swept in making me shiver. "Listen, he was the father of my children. He'd been my lover, my best friend and the love of my life since I was twenty. And, more than that, beyond all of the silly comments and put downs, he was such a good man and bloody brilliant father. There wasn't much I could fault him for, there really wasn't." Alex looked cold and sad, like a small boy that had just been told he was being sent back to the orphanage. I forced my way back into his arms and he embraced me timidly at first, but then harder until I couldn't breathe.

"Good job he's dead, or I'd be seriously worried you were going to dump me and give him another go." He said and I couldn't help but laugh. I stepped back and pushed him away.

"Daft sod!" He gave me the wonkiest grin, still looking a little downtrodden. I looped arms with him, and we carried on walking.

"So, you're a professional ghost hunter now then?" he asked after a while.

"Yep, although not a very good one I would say."

"Ben must know a bit about ghosts and how all that stuff works though, being dead and all."

"Sweet FA." I said.

"No need to be rude about it." He said before following my gaze to the grave behind him.

"No, look. Sweet Fanny Adams." How could I have forgotten about this? We both read the grave inscription in silence.

"Aged 8 years and 4 months who was cruelly murdered..." muttered Alex. I felt my stomach drop to the floor. They had said as much in the basement that day. Poor girl. "I think I remember reading something about this when I first moved here. Didn't they find her chopped up and scattered all over the Hop fields? Apparently, he gouged out her eyes. They found them the next day in the River Wey."

"Oh Christ. This is her. This is the girl that has been haunting The Crown."

"But why?" asked Alex.

"I don't know. It could be as simple as she has latched onto the little girl that is living there. But it doesn't make sense. She seems quite fond of Natalie, I don't see why she would want to scare her and her family." Alex was watching me with a weary look, as if he could sense my exhaustion.

"Maybe she's trying to protect her?" he said. It made perfect sense.

"But from what?" I shivered at the thought.

"I don't know." he said, "Come on. Let's get you home. We can have our chat another day." I was so relieved I could have cried. We turned and walked back out of the cemetery and onto the main road. When I told him I could manage the rest of the way, he tried to argue but I just held up a hand. I needed to be alone.

24
(Before)

I'd been psyching myself up all day to talk to him, but I knew it was a bad idea to pounce on him the second that he walked through the door from work. I'd tucked the newspaper into a drawer in the sideboard and cooked him his favourite tea; Shepherd's Pie. After dinner he'd put his feet up in front of the tv and the girls has escaped upstairs to do their homework, or most likely talking to their friends on their mobiles, whatever it was that teenage girls did in their bedrooms these days. I knew that the secondary schools kept them busy and challenged, so whatever they needed to do to unwind at the end of the day was absolutely fine by me. They were safe at home, so I couldn't really complain. I had peeked my head around their doors to check in on them before gathering all my fortitude and heading downstairs to have a little chat with my husband.

I sat on the sofa adjacent to him and Norbert immediately leapt onto my lap, descending into a squeaky snore that could be heard over the tv. Some brand of cookery program was on, although Ben was barely paying attention as he was frowning at his mobile which he held inches away from his face and periodically jabbed with a finger. Something was irritating him today. That wasn't a good start.

"Can't believe what they are asking for these cars." he said angrily. He was on the look-out for a new car but wanted to save a bit of cash by getting the model he wanted but a couple of years older. I suspected it was going to cost a fortune, but he managed the family finances and assured me that we could easily afford it. He needed a smarter looking car. He'd informed me that he would be overlooked for promotions if he didn't look the part and that meant getting a newer car than Steve, his best work friend/bitter rival/arch nemesis. I tried to nod and look sympathetic and interested but he didn't appear to be paying any attention to me.

"Remind me again why you aren't just buying a brand-new car? Would it not be more economical and reliable?" I asked.

"Not necessarily. And new cars are a lot more expensive. You lose half the value when you drive it off the forecourt."

"Ah, maybe I can help you there." I said trying not to sound too excited. I jumped up, attempting to dump the cat off my lap, but he dug his claws in, refusing to be shifted. I half stood for several ridiculous minutes. Any normal person would have pushed the cat off, but they would have drastically underestimated the psychotic tendencies of this formidable furry terrorist. After samba bouncing a few times he gave in and jumped down. I shuffled into the dining room and retrieved the paper from the drawer and plonked myself down next to Ben on the sofa, causing him to spill the beer he had been attempting to sip. I tried to ignore his intense irritation and unfolded the paper at the advert that I had seen.

"There's a job vacancy I've seen. This gym is looking for a marketing assistant to do their social media campaigns for them. I know I don't have any real experience as such, but I know my way around social media and I've got some great creative ideas for them already. It's only two days a week and now the girls are finally settled at secondary school, I quite fancy having a career of my own. Plus, we can use the money to get you a nice, brand new car." Easy, sold, I thought. How could he possibly argue with that logic? I looked at his face as he frowned at the newspaper I was holding in front of him. He read it deliberately slowly and my optimism waivered slightly.

"It says they are looking for someone with at least one year's experience in marketing. And presumably someone that has seen the inside of a gym at least once in their lives" he said.

"I know, but I reckon if I could just get a foot through the door, I could sell myself. I reckon I could do this, and I'd really enjoy it."

"No, I think it's a stupid idea." Deep down I'd entirely expected this reaction but foolishly I'd allowed myself to be buoyed by a futile sense of optimism. "Besides the fact that you don't fit the criteria that they are looking for, and the fact that we don't need the money, what are you going to do with the girls during the summer holidays?"

"Ah, now I've thought about that. It's only two days a week and so I was thinking between your Mum and my Mum and your annual leave..." his face was aghast.

"You want me to use my annual leave to mind the girls over the school holidays?"

"Well, not all of it, just a day or two and..."

"No, sorry Tracey, no. It's a stupid idea. Like I said we don't need the money and I need my annual leave to get some rest. I work bloody hard to keep this family. I don't want to be spending my leave running around after the girls. There's just no upside to this." he turns back to his phone in an attempt to end the conversation.

"I just fancied doing something for me for once. It's not a huge commitment and I thought it might just be a nice compromise." I tried one last time although I knew I had lost this battle.

"It can't always be about you Trace." he said without a hint of irony and I knew that the conversation was over.

I was beyond gutted. I didn't think it was being all that selfish to be doing a little something just for myself. If I had to kick around the house day after day, house-wifing I thought I might just go crazy. The major problem wasn't filling my time, between the household chores and watching films and reading books, I had no problem with boredom. What I had been trying to achieve was a bit of pride in myself. A career I could talk about and be proud of. The opportunity to make a difference somehow and somewhere, besides just washing pants and doing the ironing and taking the cat to the vets for his boosters. Don't get me wrong, I was so lucky to have had the opportunity stay at home and raise my family and enjoy supporting them, but I just needed something more. A new challenge to tax my weary brain and push myself a little. The money didn't matter really. It was just a sense of pride. Perhaps that is a bit selfish, I thought to myself, but then everything I had done for the past fourteen years had been about my family. Maybe it was time to be a little selfish.

As I was walking back to the cabinet to put the newspaper back, I spotted an advert on the other page. It was the weekly listings for the little independent cinema in town. I'd heard it was quaint but a little bit damp and smelly, but more importantly, almost always completely empty. I checked the clock and a film I quite fancied seeing was going to start in half an hour. I questioned myself; did I dare go to the cinema on my own, or is that just what weirdos do?

I walked back to the lounge.

"They're showing that film I wanted to see this evening. You know the one about the woman who's a fortune teller and gets embroiled in a murder case. Do you mind if I go see it? It starts in half an hour?" I said. He was shocked enough to look up from his phone.

"On your own?" he asked.

"Yeah, why not?" He looked at his watch.

"If you want." he said with a sigh.

"Great." I said heading for the door.

25

It was several more days than I had anticipated until I returned to The Crown Inn. Erin informed me by email that whatever I had done had worked wonders and everything seemed to have gone back to normal. I was not so sure. Mostly because I hadn't actually done anything. In fact, I was convinced that we were really in the eye of the storm. Something was going to happen but the fact I didn't know what was taking my anxiety to a new level of insanity. The girls could sense my unease and they tiptoed around the house, helping me to stay on top of the housework and cooking when I had forgotten. I found myself at times just sitting staring into space, my mind in a desperate whirl of theories, none of which seemed right. There was a very important reason why Ben and I had been dragged into this investigation, but the answer was just out of reach.

My financial woes had been temporarily mollified by a swift payment from Erin for the services provided, so convinced was she that I had resolved their issue. It was enough to see us into the New Year and bankroll Christmas, which I hastily procured in a series of frantic online purchases. The girls spent the weekend 'festivising' the house as they liked to call it. The tree was in its usual spot, erratically hung with the hodgepodge of decorations we had acquired over the years. Nothing matched, but then what fun was Christmas if your living room didn't look like it had been turned into a whore's boudoir. That was what my mum had always said anyway.

Monday morning brought with it the prospect of me bumbling around the house on my own all day. With Ben keeping a low profile and the girls at school, it was just me thinking myself into an existential crisis. I couldn't even focus long enough to get through a sentence of the book I had been reading since before Ben had died; unheard of for me. By the time Sophie, Becky and Callum clambered through the door I was climbing the walls. They barely had time to drop their school bags before I was dragging them back out the door, tempting them into town with the promise of a diabetes-inducing snack from the café at the top of town.

We settled into a table close to the front of the coffee shop, basking in the summer sun as it streamed through the floor to ceiling windows. Sophie scraped her seat across the linoleum to perch herself as close to me as possible, our forearms wedged together in a slightly claustrophobic gesture of solidarity. I appreciated it hugely but was concerned it might impinge the performance of my preferred cake shoveling arm, so I nudged her away a tiny bit and smiled at her. She grinned back and then rested her head on my shoulder. I turned to kiss the top of her head and noticed a middle-aged couple at a table opposite ours. At first glance, they appeared to be ignoring each other, his silver head turned down to study a broadsheet newspaper and her plump, wrinkled face studying a Bakewell tart as she attacked it with a dainty fork. As he turned the page, he rustled the paper to flatten the grey pages against the table, in doing so he revealed they were holding their free hands over the table, each with their arm stretched out over the tabletop. He looked up and watched her, her eyes were closed in a moment of cakey joy and as she reopened them, their eyes met. A coy smile crept across her face.

"What?" she said quietly.

"Nothing." He said and I could tell from his voice that he was grinning ear to ear.

Sophie caught me watching the scene and wrapped her arm around mine and gave it a squeeze.

"Awww, Mum." She said. "You and Dad will miss out on so much." Her voice was cracking, and Callum dove in to hug her clumsily from the other side. Becky watched the scene from the other side of the table with wide-eyed interest, not quite managing to put on her mask of indifference in time. An unguarded tear streaked down my cheek and I swiped it away hastily. I didn't want to admit to our daughters that, I wasn't sad because I thought Ben and I had missed out on a long future of mutual tenderness, because that wasn't true at all. I was sad because in all our years of marriage we had never shared such a simple and pure affectionate moment. I felt sad for what our relationship could have been but wasn't. I hugged my daughter back, managing to envelope Callum in an arm-filler of a hug and we stayed like that until the coffees and cakes arrived.

Callum made a herculean effort to lighten the mood; he was such a clown, but an adorably sweet one. He made us all guffaw, choking on crumbs of muffins and brownies as he recalled the time he was on the beach and saw what he thought was a football sail towards him from the corner of his eye. It was only once he had committed fully to kicking the ball very hard, he realised that it was in fact a seagull coming in to land. He managed to break two toes in the encounter but ultimately felt grateful he hadn't been arrested for animal cruelty. The seagull apparently had been "well pissed off" but mostly unhurt.

Pumped full of sugar and caffeine, we headed back home through the early afternoon gloom. It was already dark by the time we arrived home and found Dad waiting in his car on the driveway. It seems he'd decided I was due another trip to the cinema. Whilst the prospect of seeing Alex and getting back out of the house was extremely tempting, I felt an overwhelming need to be in the bosom of my family and found I couldn't stomach leaving the house. Alex would have been heartbroken if he'd known I had turned down the opportunity for an evening with him, but I was studiously ignoring his texts and I hoped he understood why. Besides, I thought to myself, what was the point in teasing the poor guy when we both knew nothing could ever come of it. Not now the spirit of my dearly departed husband had taken up residence in our family home once again. How awkward would that be?

Dad decided to hang around anyway and after fussing over his granddaughters, we curled up together in front of the tv to watch Only Fools and Horses reruns and drink endless cups of tea with chocolate digestives for dunking. I knew he could tell something was wrong but in true Dad form he was not prepared to talk about feelings and such nonsense. All he could offer was hugs and the kind of reassuring Dad kisses you got on the top of your head which told you that everything was going to work out just fine. After a couple of episodes, he had fallen asleep and was snoring so loud it was scaring the cat. I made myself a fresh cup of tea and sat in the conservatory, listening to the rain hammering on the roof.

"Hey." said Ben as he appeared standing over me.

"Hey." I said back and we sat together and listened to the storm outside. "I haven't seen you for a couple of days. What have you been up to?"

"Just giving you some space." he said settling opposite me on the floor where I sat with my back against the radiator feeling my bum slowly going numb on the hard laminate floor. "You ok?" he asked.

"Yep. You?"

"Still dead." he said in a dry attempt to make me smile. Instead he got a withering look, which made him smile defiantly. "Are you ready to talk to me about Alex?" he asked, and I was surprised by his gentle tone. I had expected him to be angry.

"Nothing happened." I said, "Not even a kiss. I swear to you."

"I know." he said softly.

"We are just friends." He looked at me. It was a skeptical look. "Nothing has happened!" I protested.

"I know. I know. Calm down. Your Gran Ivy told me the second I crossed over. She's been watching the whole affair with great interest." I started to protest once more, but he stopped me, "Sorry bad turn of phrase. You know what I mean." I wondered what else she had told him (the shit-stirring cow) and realised quickly it was futile to worry. Let's just assume he knows everything, I thought to myself.

My first instinct was to defend myself and my

behaviour. I wanted to tell him about all of the times that he put me down and made me feel wretched about myself. All the times it seemed as though he was trying to turn the girls to his way of thinking; that I was just some dumb old housewife with half a braincell. I knew he hadn't done it out of malice, but it had still hurt none the less. My relationship with Alex, whatever it was or had become, was a symptom of an unhappy marriage and whilst I knew that the lack of a physical relationship didn't mean I hadn't been unfaithful, I dearly wanted Ben to understand just how down and lonely I had felt for the past few years. What good would it have done though, to say all those things? I knew as well as he did, that I had been just as much to blame for the failure of our marriage as he was, such as it was.

"I know sometimes, I wasn't very good at loving you," said Ben, "but I did always love you."

"Please don't apologise. This is all my fault. I should have told you how I was feeling so we could sort things out rather than just burying my head in the sand." As we spoke, I could feel a weight I had been carrying for many years start to lift, but I still felt pitiful for betraying my husband. Nothing he said could change that or alleviate my lingering guilt.

"Tracey, look at me." I tore my gaze from the rain streaking down the window. "I can see now how I made you feel. I just didn't make you happy. No don't. It's true. I didn't and that's not because I was a shitty person, although I could have treated you so much better and you deserved to be treated so much better. We just weren't meant to be. We were never soul mates. There's no shame in that. We had a good time together, we raised a beautiful family, but you needed something more than I could give you."

"I'm sorry." I said, not because of what I had done, but because what he was saying was true and it made me ache with sadness. I had wanted for us to be happy together so badly, but sometimes it just wasn't meant to be.

"Don't be. You have nothing to be sorry for."

"I wish things had been different for us." I dragged the sleeve of my jumper across my cheeks to mop up the tears.

"Me too" he looked crestfallen. "You and the girls are going to be fine."

"And you will always be with us...won't you?" He looked at me then and I knew what he had been avoiding telling me.

"I will always be watching over you, but I don't have much time left." he said.

"Please don't leave me. Not again." Despite everything, he was still the man that had been at my side since I was twenty years old. I had thought when he appeared to me that day in front of the car, I'd had a reprieve. I didn't imagine for a minute I would have to say goodbye a second time.

"Not just yet. Don't worry Trace, everything will be fine." he smiled and looked over my shoulder. My Dad had appeared at the patio doors, rubbing his eyes. He was holding out his empty cup to me.

"One more for the road, eh love?" he said. Just as I was lifting myself stiffly off the floor, my mobile rang.

"It's Erin" Ben said before I'd had the chance to answer.

"Tracey! It's kicked off again here." she sounded frantic. "We need you back here now, is there any chance?" I looked to Dad, it was a big ask of him but the desperate tone to Erin's voice made me feel I couldn't abandon her now.

"Hang on," I pressed the phone to my chest, "Dad, there's an urgent problem at work. I don't suppose you would mind the girls for a bit while I nip out?" He looked uncertain. The previous incident with the gas fire had left him shaken and doubting himself. I shouted up the stairs to Sophie, "Any chance you can look after your Grandad while I pop out to work?" Dad grinned and nudged my arm.

"Cheeky."

26

Within seconds I was out the front door, cheeks burning against the arctic air, run-walking to The Crown Inn. As I turned into the main road, I saw a small figure standing by the lychgate to the cemetery. It was far too late for a child that age to be out on her own, so I know instantly that it was Fanny. As I got closer, I could see the terror in her face.

"Run." she was shouting, and I broke into the fastest run I could manage. I dreaded to think what the passing cars must be thinking of this chunky thighed middle-aged woman waddling along the road. My path followed around the edge of the church, which was brightly illuminated against the dark night sky, courtesy of the stained-glass windows, brightly lit by the fake LED candles flickering fraudulently within. As I turned the corner the inn came into view and my stomach dropped to my knees. The blue flashing lights of several police cars lit up the dark street. I sprint-wobbled the rest of the way.

As I got to the door, a young policeman tried to block my entry. My God, I'm too late I thought. I felt like I was going to be sick.

"I'm Tracey," I gasped in the cold air and it hurt my lungs. I had to bend over and catch my breath. The young man guarding the door watched me expressionless. When I finally had enough breath to continue, I said, "Erin called me and asked me to come urgently." Nope, out of breath again already. The policeman, who actually looked to be only about twelve years old despite being approximately two foot taller than me, turned away and muttered into his police radio. After a mumbled crackling response, which I heard but couldn't discern any actual English words from, PC Manchildface stepped aside to let me in.

I rushed into the bar where I found a calmer scenario than I had anticipated. Erin was slouched over one of the tables in the centre of the room, a white tissue clenched tight in her fist. Her hair was scraped back from her pale face into a high ponytail and she seemed to have aged a decade since I had last seen her, wrinkles criss-crossing her forehead and stretching out from the corners of her tear blotched eyes. Beside her a female police officer, with a dour expression, her mouth pinched up like a cat's bum, was patting Erin's back awkwardly in what I presumed was an attempt at consolation. Sat opposite her was another policeman, who looked so unremarkable he could have been a standard issue police-robot. At the bar Matt sat rigidly on a bar stool, as if every bone in his body was locked tight in a cocktail of angst and fury. As I barged into the room, they all turned to look at me. I spotted Ben's spirit hiding in a dark corner of the room. His face was grim.

"Natalie has gone missing." he said.

"Natalie's gone missing." I repeated, more to clarify what I was failing to grasp.

"See…" said Erin, blowing her nose noisily, "I told you she was good." PC Catbumface looked dubious and her colleague eyeballed me with thinly veiled contempt.

"Robin has gone too, but they haven't noticed yet." added Ben.

"Robin is gone too." I said urgently. Before he could be stopped Matt rushed out of the room, closely pursued by the PC-bot. We heard the sound of a door being kicked in from the floor above us. All was silent for a moment and then footsteps thundered back down the stairs towards us. Matt looked pale with shock when he reappeared in the bar.

"Everything is gone. He's cleared out." PC Catbumface spoke urgently into her police radio. Erin was sat in a state of shock, mouth gaping and unable to speak. I put an arm around her shoulder.

"We'll find her." I said firmly and shook her slightly. "Listen to me Erin, we will find her." She couldn't speak and just blinked through the tears.

"Ben, can you find her?" I asked, no longer caring if anyone thought I looked a bit nuts for speaking to an empty corner of the room. None of the police had bothered to introduce themselves to me so I considered myself a non-entity to them.

"I don't know." he looked panicked and we were reminded once again just how far out of our depth we were. Beside Ben a small figure started to appear. A small pale hand took his.

"I'll show you…" said Fanny and they both disappeared.

All that was left for me to do was to sit tight until they could help. Erin was sobbing into her arms as she attempted to give a description of Robin to the PC-

Bot and Matt was pacing furiously up and down the bar. Something snapped in him and he charged towards the door.

"Where are you going?" my voice was shrill. I was not coping with the situation very well. All I could think about was what if this was one of my girls.

"To find my daughter." he shouted. PC-Bot moved forward to object, but Matt had disappeared through the door before he had a chance. A fresh wail of despair came from the hunched-up lump of Erin. I wondered frantically if there was anything I could have done to prevent this. Had Fanny known that this was going to happen? And if so, why the hell hadn't she told us, we could have persuaded Erin and Matt to get rid of him. But then I thought back to my last time at the Inn and how defensive Erin had been of him. She wouldn't have been convinced. I was sure of it then. I remembered suddenly Matt's angry exchange with Robin that day. He must have caught Robin in Natalie's room not Erin's as I had originally assumed. If that man could have pulled himself out of his drunken self-pity, I might have stood a chance of getting Robin away from her. I felt the burn of shame. I had assumed that Erin and Robin had been having an affair. Just as the panic in my chest was rising to a crescendo, I sensed Ben and Fanny reappearing in the corner of the bar.

"She's alive." He said urgently. "They are at The Flood Meadows. You have to go now!" he shouted, and I felt his panic. Ben never raised his voice.

"They are at the Flood Meadows." I blurted out to the police officers in the room. They looked taken aback for a moment but then went back to ignoring me. "Did you hear me?" I shouted, "You have to get officers to the flood meadows."

"Listen, Tracey is it?" said the PC-Bot in a condescending tone, "We have a process to follow in the case of a missing child. This is an extremely sensitive incident. You have to trust that we are doing all that we can to find the little girl." I wanted to slap him very hard.

"But I know where she is, just send someone down there. Please!" I was practically on my knees begging this man. "You have to go now before she gets hurt!" The PC-Bot narrowed his eyes at me.

"May I ask Madam how you seem to know so much about the whereabouts of the little girl?" he stepped towards me. Shit.

"Tracey, you have to get out of here now!" shouted Ben. Talk about pointing out the fucking obvious. I took a cautious step backwards to test how the policeman would react. He was on guard and flinched his hand towards his handcuffs as I moved. Crap, Fuck, bollocks I thought.

I saw a movement behind him. Fanny had moved towards the door at the opposite end of the room and was slowly pulling it open. The policeman could see me looking over his shoulder but refused to be fooled and kept his eyes trained on me. I could almost see the beads of sweat gathering at his temple. I looked to Fanny, she nodded to me and slammed the door with such ferocity I could have sworn the entire building shook with the force. The precise second that she did so, I legged it. I was through the door and pushing past the PC Manchildface in an instant and pegging it down the road. It was a proper knees-to-chest run and there was no dignity to it, but I was beyond having any dignity. Pure unadulterated terror for what could be happening to Natalie was fuelling my chubby body.

27

I had a good minute's advantage, before I heard the police shouts behind me.

"There she is!" and I knew they were close behind me. I needed the advantage on account of being old and fat; there was no way I could outrun Alton's finest. Feet thundered on the pavement behind me as I ran down the dark hill, turning right. Without the downward momentum, I struggled to keep up my pace, but I was soon tearing up Tanhouse Lane and into the darkness of the flood meadows. They were gaining on me as I hurled myself into the darkness, realising in a panic that I had no idea where she could be. I needed Ben. I turned left to run along the river and crouched panting in the undergrowth until I saw the two dark shadows of the police officers appearing. Their police radios were cracking frantically as they swept a torchlight across the area, narrowly avoiding me.

The flood meadows consisted of two large fields, interspersed with trees and the River Wey running along its southern flank. It was hemmed in on the remaining three sides by housing estates, including my own. The area was vast, but thankfully pitch black and I could hear the police calling for back up. In a sense this was mission accomplished, I had managed to get the police here, but I felt a pressing urgency to find Natalie, whilst not getting caught myself first. I waited for the two policemen to head off in separate directions before I rose from my hiding place and looked around frantically. I spotted Fanny further along the river, signalling urgently for me to follow her. I cast one more look around and then treaded quietly along the muddy path. As I reached her she disappeared and instantly reappeared further up the path, her tiny form shimmering slightly in the dim moonlight. My heart was thumping so hard in my ears I could barely hear anything other than that and my own gasping breath.

The next time Fanny appeared she was the other side of the river. The ice-cold water seeped through my trainers and I gasped. Within seconds I couldn't feel anything below my ankles. Fanny was looking ever more urgent as I clambered out onto the muddy verge on the other side of the river. I crept through the overgrown scrub, weaving in amongst the willow and alder trees, until the sound of a man's voice made me freeze. My eyes were just starting to adjust to the darkness, and I could just about make out two figures, standing in clearing. I edged closer.

"It will be more fun if you wait for her to wake." An unfamiliar voice said, making my blood freeze. I continued moving forward, aware of every crackle of the dead, dried leaves under my feet, certain they would hear me coming a mile off. I took another step and my foot caught on a rogue hazel branch. I tumbled forward, landing on my face in a clearing with an almighty crash. Looking up from the leaves that barely cushioned my fall, I saw the tiny form of Natalie curled up on the ground in front of me. Crawling forward on all fours, I pulled her onto her back, anxiously checking for a pulse. She was pale and still but the tiny thump of her heartbeat against my fingers overwhelmed me with relief. I looked up from the little girl to find Robin and a man dressed all in black standing over me, their faces a mixture of annoyance and bemusement.

"Trace..." Ben had appeared behind me on the edge of the clearing. His voice was sharp and tense, "he's got a knife Trace." The nine-inch blade glinted in Robin's hand. I imagined he was wondering what this fat middle aged woman was doing interfering with his fun.

"Robin listen to me. It's not too late to stop this." I started to scramble to my feet, staying bent low to grab Natalie. "There are police all over this area looking for you...well me technically, but either way they are going to find us any minute." I didn't think I could talk him round but if I could make enough noise the police might find us in time. Robin sneered at me and took a step forward.

"Well, I'd better do it fast then hadn't I?" he said.

"Cut the old woman first." hissed the man in the black suit.

"Old!" I shouted indignantly. What a nerve! They looked at me in irritation but then turned back to one another.

"Then we can take our time with the girl." The man in black continued grinning a black toothed affair that failed to reach his jet-black eyes. Robin took another step forward. I fumbled in my pocket for my mobile. The glare of the screen burned my eyes as I fumble for the music app I had Ben put on there for me last year. There was no time to find anything more fitting to the current circumstances in my playlists so I just hit play and the introduction bars to the extended version of Boney M's Rasputin blared into the darkness. I took advantage of the Robin's shock to whack up the volume. If the police couldn't track us down now, we had no hope.

Ben suddenly launched himself at the man in the black suit and the two spirits scuffled in the mud. Taking advantage of the distraction caused by the kerfuffle, I grabbed Natalie, her tiny body felt so small and light in my arms, and I turned to run. Robin howled and I knew he was after us. Every single muscle in my body hurt but the adrenaline was pumping, and I made it to the river, Boney M still blaring from the phone in my pocket. Once in the river, my foot slipped on a stone and I fell forwards, managing to hurl the tiny unconscious body to the river bank, praying I hadn't hurt her in the process. I sailed forwards, gasping as the cold engulfed my entire body. Dragging myself out of the water, my clothes weighing twice what they had been and shivering viciously, I turned to see Robin appear at the other bank and launch himself in the water. Behind me I could see the light of the police torches diverging and frantically bobbing in my direction. I couldn't run anymore, but I had to keep Robin away from her.

Groping around in the undergrowth I found a small rock. I turned and hurled it into Robin's face. The pebble, as it turned out, miraculously landed directly between his eyes and bounced off his forehead.

"Ow." he said rubbing his forehead. Wildly grasping at the muddy bank, I found a couple more stones and hurled them in his direction. He flinched and dodged a few but a bigger one caught him on the side of his arm. 'Ouch. Stop that." he shouted. Despite my barrage of tiny missiles, he staggered forward through the knee-deep river and was on top of me before I could move. Pinning me to the bank with his body weight, he pushed my head back into the mud. Anchoring the palm of his hand under my chin, I felt him push with tremendous strength so that my neck was bare to the moonlight. I saw the glint of the knife as he raised it high above his head.

A large black boot appeared above my head, sailing out of the dark, hoofing Robin hard in the face. It caught him by surprise causing him to rock back. He shook his head and I heard the knife fall into the river with a splash. The boot reappeared and thumped him a second time but harder and he too landed in the river. I gasped in the breath I had been holding and struggled up to see PC Manchildface stood over me.

"You alright?" he shouted down at me. I pointed to the little body lying a little further along on the river bank where I had thrown her. I watched as he checked her and slid his coat off to cover her.

"Child has been found. She's unconscious but breathing. We're going to need an ambulance." He said into his radio. As I slipped into unconsciousness, it occurred to me that he didn't just look like a twelve-year-old, he sounded like one too. Bless his little cottons.

28

Later I could only feel pity for the poor policeman whose job it had been to fish me out of the river. I was only told about this later whilst in my hospital bed. I'd been cuffed to the side of the bed until I could explain my involvement in the little girl's disappearance and how I came to know where she was. Ah...shit. I'd asked how Natalie was, but they had refused to tell me. I'd begged Ben to come and tell me what was going on. What was I supposed to do? I needed to know he was ok because the last time I had seen him he was wrestling with the man in black. It seemed I had been abandoned by all spiritual beings and I had no choice but to be completely honest.

"I knew where she was because the ghost of Fanny Adams told me." I said. The officer looked me dead in the eye and I just stared straight back, which unsettled him somewhat. Clearly, he was used to dealing with actual criminals.

"I see." he said noting something down in his notebook, possibly just the one word: mental. "And do you see ghosts often then Mrs Cringle?" his tone was mocking.

"Actually, yes I do. It's my job."

"I see." he said again, the sarcastic quality to his voice was both unmistakable and tiresome. As he was scribbling in his notebook, a shimmer in the corner the room caught my eye. A short lady with dark glasses and a dumpy frame appeared. Her hair was piled up on top her head, forming a curious pyramid of deep red curls, interlaced with grey. She smiled at me and stood behind the officer's chair. He shivered as if he had caught a breeze, but then shrugged it off. The spirit woman ruffled his hair.

"Oh! He's cut off his curls. Shame..." she said pouting.

"There's an old lady here..." I started and she flung a mutinous look at me, "Errr, slightly older lady here. I think she might be a grandmother to you." I said. Officer Curls raised his eyes but kept his head pointed down at the page, in a gesture which suggested he couldn't even be bothered to humour me right now.

"I'm his nanny Nora." she whispered to me unnecessarily as he couldn't hear her either way. I fixed Officer Curls with a glare.

"She is saying that she is your Nanny Nora and it's a shame you cut off your curls." Instantly Officer Curls sat bolt upright in his chair, his back ramrod straight. Just as quick he leered at me, as if his body was reacting but his face was taking longer to catch up. It seemed he would take a little more convincing. I looked to Nanny Nora, hoping she would oblige, and as Nannies are often wont to do, she told me all about his childhood, so much so I worried she would not stop talking. All the while Officer Curls unwavering gaze was scrutinizing me as he silently diagnosed my psychological wellbeing as unstable.

"Ok," I said to Nora, imploring her to stop and I

looked back to Officer Curls. "She is telling me about how you used to help her bake Coffee Kisses in the kitchen when you were younger and how your family begged her to teach you a new recipe because when you got home you just insisted on making them again and again. She also said you've been asking your mum about the small scar on your forehead and she didn't seem to know where it had come from. Your Nanny says that you tripped up the concrete steps to her house when you were a toddler and bashed your forehead on the step above. Although she doesn't know why your mum can't remember this because she definitely told her." Nanna Nora started talking over me before I could relay all of the information back to Officer Curls, although I noticed with a note of satisfaction that the smug grin had slowly slid off his face as I had been talking. When Nora had finished talking, I turned to her.

"I'm not saying that to him" I said but she was not taking no for an answer. "Fine, ok. Right, she says you have to stop doing that thing with the sock. It's disgusting. Get yourself a girlfriend." Officer Curls whimpered quietly and blushed a delightfully scarlet red. He jumped out of his chair and muttered something about speaking to another colleague and all but ran out of my hospital room.

"I'm not sure that has helped my cause." I said to Nora as her spirit started to fade.

"Nah, but it was fun to see his face." she cackled with laughter as she disappeared. I smiled to myself and lay back in the bed. Reality hit hard very suddenly. Christmas was only a week away and I couldn't let the girls spend their first Christmas since their father died without me too. What do they even do with people accused of child abduction? Would I rot in a jail cell until they were able to prove my innocence, or would I have to find bail money? I'd never been so much as been arrested, let along languished in jail. More to the point, I thought frantically, where in the hell was Ben? I desperately needed his support, but I hadn't seen him since the fight at the Flood Meadows. A fresh anxiety hit, and I realised just how little I knew about the spirit world and the capabilities of malign entities. Everything suddenly seemed a bit bleak and I just wanted to sleep then cry or cry then sleep. I was too tired to decide which.

The door to my room opened and Officer ManChildFace entered the room, walking up to the side of my hospital bed. This is it, I thought, I'm going to be formally arrested.

"Let's get these off you." he said as he unlocked the handcuffs that had me attached to the bed. I rubbed the red marks on my wrists, whilst trying to hold back the tears of relief. I could hug you Officer Manchildface I thought to myself.

"Has something happened? Is there any news on Natalie?"

"There is. She is awake and absolutely fine. She has told us that the young man that was arrested had given her a drink of hot milk that made her sleepy. She vaguely remembers him carrying her away, but not much else." He seemed to hear a noise in the corridor and paused to listen for a second, which told me he was probably giving me more information that he should have been. "In any case, we have a pretty comprehensive testimony from Robin which indicates that he worked entirely alone. All charges against you are to be dropped and as soon as the doctors have given you the all clear you are free to go." I threw myself back on my pillow and sobbed with relief.

"Thank god. Thank you." My tears seemed to make Officer Manchildface distinctly uncomfortable, so I tried to pull myself together. "Thank you so much for showing up the last minute and kicking that evil bastard in the face."

"Twice." he said with some pride.

"Yes, indeed. Right in the face too. Nice work officer."

"You are welcome." he said with a nod of the head, "Incidentally, Boney M was a bold choice of music..."

"It was just the next song in my playlist." I admitted somewhat sheepishly.

"And that is a bold admission." He said and then he turned and walked out of the door. Cheeky, I thought. There's nothing wrong with a bit of vintage disco pop music.

I allowed myself a short snooze while I waited for a nurse or doctor to show up. As a result, I ended up sleeping for three hours, having been forgotten in the general melee of A&E. When someone did finally show up, I begged to be given my phone; Dad and the girls would be beside themselves although I hadn't quite figured out how I would get home from the hospital. I was amazed that I was still alive after having been dunked and bashed about all evening. Thankfully there were no missed calls, but there were a dozen anxious texts from Dad and my customary five text messages from Alex. Before Ben died, we would spend entire days engaged in text volleys. Just two friends chatting, we never seemed to run out of things to say to one another. But then Ben had gone and died, and it made things difficult for me. The first couple of days his messages were a comfort although I seldom found the words with which to respond. Then, when Ben's ghost had started showing up, I felt I couldn't even check my phone for fear that Ben would be looking over my shoulder and I would be caught out. Once a day I would find a quiet spot to check what Alex had had to say and it would give me a brief respite from grieving and a welcome distraction. Today's messages were much the same.

He started by saying he'd enjoyed our walk the other day and suggesting we should do it more often. Next, he told me that he'd put his back out carrying some older films from the archive into the screening room ahead of the Sunday afternoon flashback. His third message was just the word ouch followed by a sad face. Next, he informed me that the drugs do in fact work and he was going to have a little lie down. His last message at 8.35pm simply said "I miss you". I checked the time; it was quarter past one in the morning and he would almost certainly have been in a bed for a while.

I fired off a response: Don't suppose you could help out a damsel in distress?

I didn't expect a response, so I set about getting out of the hospital gown and back into my clothes which it seemed some kind person had dried for me. I was just struggling into my jeans when my phone rang.

It took Alex a suspiciously short amount of time to drive to Basingstoke Hospital where I was waiting outside the A&E reception with a repulsive cup of vending machine coffee. Instead of pulling up and letting me jump in, he ground to a halt, switched off the engine and leapt out of the car. I was in his arms in seconds. He smelled amazing and the warmth of his body against mine was heavenly. I felt his soft lips brush the top of my head again and again. All I could do was squeeze him hard and hope he could feel the rush of love I was feeling for him. I briefly considered if this would be the right time for our first kiss, but I was fairly certain I looked like a truck, so I kept my face turned down and buried into his soft jumper.

"Is Ben here?" he whispered into my ear. I shook my head into his chest. He ran his hand down my cheek and gently pulled my face up. We were nose-to-nose under the dim lights of the hospital in the fresh winter night. I let myself look into his eyes and found in there, understanding and affection. "You're so beautiful." he stroked his thumb across my cheek again. I rose up onto the balls of my feet and our lips met for the first time. His lips were tender and warm. I pressed gently into him and we stayed like that until the cold threatened to make us shiver. He pulled away from me, stroked my hair back off my face and kissed me once more on my forehead.

I fell asleep several times on the way back home, jumping back up in my seat as I felt myself drift off, not wanting to miss a single second with him. Nothing had changed really and yet everything felt different. I was still a recently bereaved widow and we were still going to have to sit out a respectful period of mourning regardless of whether we had Ben's blessing or not. We could still be friends though, good friends at that and whatever happened behind closed doors, well that was our business anyway. Although I had to admit to finding the idea of Alex seeing me naked utterly terrifying. Twenty years ago, I would have whipped everything off without a second's thought and jumped straight onto him, but now there were stretch marks and lumpy bits and hair where there shouldn't be and sometimes no hair where there should be some. Growing old was a confusing mess of disappointment, but I was certain of the fact that if there was one person who could tolerate all of my perfect imperfections and wobbly bits, it was Alex.

We arrived back at my house just past two thirty. The street was empty and dark. Alex parked the car on the road blocking the drive. He kept the engine running so that the heating would keep us warm. He took my hand in his, stroking it with his thumb. I didn't want to move out of his car. I didn't want the night of our first kiss to end; it was just an unending urge to be close to him.

"What now?" he finally said the words that I had been dreading.

"I can't answer that Alex, you know that." I sighed and he looked pained.

"Sorry, sorry, I'm not trying to put pressure on you. I swear. I just..."

"It's ok, don't apologise. You're not putting pressure on me, honestly. I wish I could give you more, but we just have to be patient. No-one is going to be ready for me to bring home a new boyfriend, nor will they be for a long time. I will understand if you don't want to wait..."

"No, don't say that." he lifted my hands to his mouth and kissed them, "I will wait for years and years. Forever, if I have to. Tracey, I love you and I would give anything to be with you." He looked at me so intensely then. It wasn't a stare that left me self-conscious or intimidated. It made me feel beautiful for the first time in a very long time.

"We can still be close friends." I said. It's not

what I wanted to be saying. I wanted to urge him to run away with me so we didn't have to waste another second of our lives not being with each other, but I couldn't. "I love you too." He reached his hand behind my head and pulled me close and we kissed. I wondered when the last time was that I felt a kiss as wonderful as this, if ever. My chest was aching, as if there was an invisible chain between his heart and mine, pulling us closer together. Each time I pulled away from him, it hurt. My hand snaked up behind his head and stroked the short hair on the back of his head, delicately pushing it up and down. When we stopped kissing to breathe, we rested our foreheads together, noses nestled against each other. I closed my eyes and wished I could stay with him like that forever. It was only the thought that the sooner I went to sleep, the closer we would be to the day we could be together as a couple, that gave me the strength to sit back in the car seat. I pulled open the car door and stepped out into the cold. I couldn't look back or say another word.

He watched me walk to the front door and I turned to wave before stepping into the house. Only then did I hear the car rev and drive away.

29

Ben never did reappear after that day at the flood meadows. I did receive one other visitor from the other side. My Nan Ivy appeared to me a week later while I was loading up the washing machine. At that point it had been a while since I had had any contact with the dead, so it rather took me by surprise, and I swore loudly as I doused the cat in laundry detergent. After making me apologise for my bad language and animal abuse, Nan explained that Ben was on the other side recovering his energy. She told me that on the night Natalie disappeared he had battled with the man in the black suit, which had cost him significant energy. She also told me that the man in the black suit had been Frederick Baker, the man who had violently murdered and dismembered poor little Fanny Adams before gouging out her eyes and impaling her head on a hop pole to be found by one of the locals who had joined the hunt for the little girl. She told me that Ben would be able to come back eventually to visit us but that he was able to watch over us until then. I'd cried for a long time after her visit, even whilst I attempted to wash the detergent out of Norbert's fur, which took a lot longer than you would expect. He was still foaming at the mouth a week after, as he tried to clean the last of the soap off himself.

Over the course of the year, Alex and I kept up our weekly trysts at the cinema, on occasion feeling brave enough to skip the film altogether and just spending the evening in Alex's flat above the cinema, where we would laze in bed for hours. Despite my fears, I loved to let him feel my naked body against his, letting his strong hands wander wherever he wanted them to. Eventually over time I started to let myself look in the mirror again and gradually I stopped loathing what I saw. I tried to imagine how I must look to Alex, based on the things he told me about my beautiful face, my soft cheeks, my stunning smile. One day, several months later I had looked in the mirror and realised that staring back at me was a surprisingly attractive, sexy woman, who could perhaps do with losing a few pounds. Well, Rome wasn't built in a day and I had found myself gaining a little weight recently. Mostly due to Alex's insistence on constantly feeding me. I took it as the ultimate sign of affection and nurturing to feed the person you love as opposed to some sinister feeder relationship.

We started going for long walks around town, careful to avoid the main roads and pathways where anyone who knew me might see us and draw conclusions. Between that and the sex sessions in his flat, I was actually doing a lot to mitigate the lavish meals he cooked for me and the one a day Yorkie habit he had developed. Once the last cheque from The Crown Inn had cleared, I had brought my career as a medium and ghost hunter to a grateful and abrupt end. Although, unaware of my break with the spirit world, PC Curls still crossed the street hastily when he saw me out on his beat. Early in the new year I'd seen a part time job advertised in the window of the second-hand book shop opposite the cinema. They had snapped me up, to my shock. It may have been my encyclopedic knowledge of local history and passion for modern women's fiction that clinched it. So, four days a week I was right under the nose of the love of my life and he would sneak in at lunch time to sit in the dusty room at the back of the shop and share a pot of soup, finished off with half a Yorkie bar. We talked like best friends without a break, kissed like new lovers and occasionally had a sneaky fumble if we thought we could get away with it.

It seemed peculiar that everything should seem so right, but never did we ever get a sense that things between us might not work out. We took it as sign from fate that we were just meant to be. In early September I sat the girls down and tentatively approached the subject of me going out on a date with a good friend. The idea of speaking to them had been filling me with immense anxiety so I was both relieved and a little miffed when they both seemed nonplussed even flippant about it.

"Yeah, whatever. What's for tea?" said Becky. Sophie had wanted to lecture me at length on the importance of me moving on and being happy for me, now I had given up the best of my years raising my family. The cheek!

When the night finally came, the girls fussed over my hair and make up for hours. It took physical restraint to stop Sophie from waxing off my eyebrows and drawing them back in the shape of upside-down Nike logos with a black pencil. Both girls had then stood in horror watching me plucking indiscriminately at my face with a pair of tweezers. I later heard Becky talking to her sister.

"When I get to the age where I have to spend hours in front of the mirror plucking off my chin hairs and looking sad, I want to be euthanised." I didn't hear Sophie's response, but I suspect she had agreed to the pact. Just you wait girls, I thought. Middle age is full of fun surprises like this.

When Alex arrived on the doorstep, I felt like a brutalised turkey on Christmas morning. The second I saw his face though, none of it mattered. I could have been wearing my fluffy penguin jim jams, with two days greasy hair and a big zit on my nose, he still would have looked at me like I was the most incredible creature he had ever laid eyes on. I made a mental note, never to urge him to get an eye test, but then mentally chastised myself. Enough of that bollocks, I thought. I'm allowed to feel like I'm good enough.

We looked at each other, him stood on the doorstep and me in the doorway like a couple of teenagers on a first date and then we burst out laughing. He offered out an arm for me to take.

"Shall we?" he said. I took his arm and stepped to his side.

"Yes lets." I said.

The End

ABOUT THE AUTHOR

Sarah Branch lives with her partner, in a wonky cottage overlooking an ancient graveyard, in the heart of Alton, Hampshire. At any given time, there are up to four of the offspring they have produced between them squeezed into the tiny house, plus a neurotic sheepdog and a psychotic black cat.

This is Sarah's second novel. Her first novel, Hope, is available on Amazon.